'Would you tell ▮

  'A *story*?'

  'Yes. The story of how you got that painting by Neville Windrush. The story about the bullet hole.'

  Stanley Buckle didn't say a word, but a smile spread slowly across his face. It was the same smile Sally had noticed in the photograph album. In all those years it hadn't changed.

Reviews of Richard Kidd's first novel, *The Giant Goldfish Robbery*:

'A refreshingly old-fashioned adventure . . . the best adventure story for seven- to ten-year-olds so far this year' *Literary Review*

'A witty contemporary adventure story' *Financial Times*

'A beautifully paced debut . . . the refreshing thing about this novel is its emphasis on action rather than subtext' *The Times Educational Supplement*

Also by Richard Kidd
and published in Corgi Yearling

THE GIANT GOLDFISH ROBBERY

RICHARD KIDD

This book is to be returned on or before the last date
stamped below

27 11 16

Learning Resource Centre
City of Westminster College – Paddington Centre
Paddington Green, London W2 1NB
020 7258 2738

Please note: fines for items returned after the due date
are charged at **10p per day per item**

CORGI YEARLING BOOKS

To Lucy and all my friends on Hoy

DEADLY FAMOUS
A CORGI YEARLING BOOK : 0 440 864135

First publication in Great Britain

PRINTING HISTORY
Corgi Yearling edition published 2001

1 3 5 7 9 10 8 6 4 2

Set in 12/16pt Palatino by
Phoenix Typesetting, Ilkley, West Yorkshire

Corgi Yearling Books are published by Transworld Publishers,
61–63 Uxbridge Road, London W5 5SA,
a division of The Random House Group Ltd,
in Australia by Random House Australia (Pty) Ltd,
20 Alfred Street, Milsons Point, Sydney, NSW 2061,
in New Zealand by Random House New Zealand Ltd,
18 Poland Road, Glenfield, Auckland 10,
and in South Africa by Random House (Pty) Ltd,
Endulini, 5A Jubilee Road, Parktown 2193, South Africa

Made and printed in Great Britain by
Cox & Wyman Ltd, Reading, Berks

PROLOGUE

Look Through Any Window

Nothing's ever quite what it seems, thought Sally, stretching out her arm and touching the cold glass of the window with her fingertips, not even this glass. She gave it a tap, remembering how someone had once told her that glass wasn't really a solid, but a very, *very* slow-moving liquid. You could tell this was true, because really old glass was always thicker at the bottom than the top.

She let her fingers slide down and listened to the high-pitched *squeak*. This didn't even look like a window. You were meant to be able to see through windows. This was a black mirror, squirming with silver raindrops that swarmed out of the darkness and pressed themselves against the glass.

It had been raining off and on, but mostly 'on', for five whole days now. Not just ordinary everyday 'pitter-patter' rain. This was serious rain, the kind that 'came down in stair-rods', as Granny said, the kind that flooded fields and drowned sheep and crept into people's houses when they were asleep.

That's what had happened to Sally. She'd gone to bed on Monday night just before the River Windrush burst its banks and on Tuesday morning she'd stood at the top of the stairs at 29 River Road, with her mum and dad, and watched as their brand-new digital telly had floated out of the front room, through into the kitchen . . . then sank. They were rescued shortly afterwards and now they were all living up at Gran Buckle's house, higher up the hill, until the river went down and things got back to normal. Sally's gran took it all in her stride. 'It's not nearly as bad as the Great Flood of sixty-six,' was all she'd said. Nothing shook Gran, she was unflappable.

It was Thursday night, two days after the rescue. Sally's mum was out at keep-fit, Sally's dad was reading the newspaper and her Uncle Stanley was stretched out in front of the fire, fast asleep.

Jet lag, thought Sally.

Uncle Stanley was Mum's older brother. He'd arrived the day the rains began. 'Brought the good weather with him,' joked Gran. He'd flown more than halfway round the world, all the way from New Zealand, to go to some fancy exhibition of paintings at the Tate Gallery in London. He wasn't an artist though, he was a bee-keeper with the biggest honey farm in New Zealand: *Buckle's Blossom Honey – Seven Deliciously Different Varieties – Spread All Over The Antipodes.*

Mum called him 'The Mr Bee of Down Under'. He didn't look like a bee-keeper, but then, what did a bee-keeper look like anyway? Sally hadn't a clue. In fact, she didn't have much of an idea about her Uncle Stanley, full stop. It was the first time she'd ever met him and he was a bit of a mystery.

'You look miles away,' said Gran. 'How about a nice cup of cocoa before bedtime?'

'Mmmmm, sounds good.'

'I'll see what I can do then.'

Gran left the room and Sally glanced across at the stack of old photograph albums they'd been looking through. It was fun doing things like that with Gran, because Gran remembered being there as if it was yesterday. She knew all the stories that went with the pictures. Most of the stories were happy, after all, that's why people took photographs, to help them remember the happy times. But some turned out to be sad, such as the one of the big man in the checked shirt, with a little girl on his shoulders and a boy standing beside him with a pair of binoculars round his neck. Underneath it said, *Wales, 1962.* The little girl was Sally's mum, Rachel, and the boy was her brother, Stanley. The big man with the checked shirt was their dad, Sally's grandfather, who Sally never met, because he'd died of a burst appendix just two weeks after that photograph was taken. That's why it was sad.

There was one album left they hadn't looked at. Sally began at the back, turning the pages, travelling backwards through time: 1969, 1968 . . . There was her gran, looking really glamorous in a white dress with big black spots all over it. Underneath someone had written, *The day we went to London, July, 1967.* Sally smiled and kept turning the pages until another photograph caught her eye. It wasn't like the others. It was all creased and dog-eared, as if someone had been carrying it round in their pocket before they'd decided to stick it in the album.

It was of a boy about her age standing next to a big man with round black glasses that made him look like an owl. The man was wearing a baggy jumper with some kind of pattern on it and they were both standing beside a white beehive. Sitting on top of the beehive was what looked like a smallish lion, but was probably a very large ginger cat. Underneath someone had written, *Stanley with Neville Windrush and Vincent, The Old Mill, August, 1966.* There was something else, an equally well-thumbed photograph of John Wayne, *Number thirty-two in a series of fifty, 'Stars Of The Silver Screen'*.

Sally had never met Neville Windrush, but she'd heard of him – who hadn't? He was definitely the most famous person that had ever lived in Welford. Probably as famous as John Wayne. She'd read somewhere recently that he was the most famous painter alive in Britain today, except he spent most of his time abroad. There was going to be a huge exhibition of his paintings opening tomorrow night at the Tate Gallery in London. That's what her Uncle Stanley had travelled half way round the world to go to, and now, because of these stupid floods, he was probably going to miss it.

His invitation card was propped up on the mantelpiece. Sally tiptoed across the room, picked it up and took it back over to the table with the photograph albums.

The Director of The Tate Gallery
requests the pleasure of the company of
Stanley Buckle Esq. (and guest)
at the opening party for the exhibition of paintings by

Neville Windrush

Black Tie; Champagne   *R.S.V.P.*

On the other side was a picture of one of Neville Windrush's paintings. It looked like it was meant to be a massive chimney, or something, collapsing into the sea. She didn't understand it. It made her feel dizzy. The actual painting belonged to Uncle Stanley. It was his. The Tate Gallery had asked to borrow it especially for the exhibition. They said it was a very important painting. It must have been to have fetched it all the way from New Zealand, thought Sally.

There was something else about the painting, something odd. It had a small hole in the top right-hand corner. You could just about make it out on the card and underneath the picture it said: *The Old Man of Hoy; 1967; 48ins. by 30ins.; Oil on Canvas; Private Collection. (This painting suffered minor damage shortly after its completion but, at the specific request of the artist, it was never repaired.)*

'Penny for your thoughts,' offered Gran, setting down a tray with two steaming mugs of cocoa.

'The hole,' murmured Sally, from what seemed like a long way away.

'Beg your pardon?'

'The painting – the one the Tate Gallery borrowed from Uncle Stanley – the one on this card. It's got a little round hole in the top right-hand corner.'

'Oh, you mean the bullet hole,' said Gran, matter-of-factly.

'The *what*?'

'The bullet hole,' repeated Gran. 'I take it you've not heard the famous story of how your Uncle Stanley came by that painting.'

'No,' said Sally in a daze.

'He's a dark horse is our Stanley,' said Gran, 'still waters, etc. But it's too long a story and too late to start telling it now. Besides, it's Stanley's story and he should be the one to tell it. You should ask him yourself. Tomorrow.'

When Sally woke the next morning the rain had stopped and the sun was shining. It was ten o'clock. She'd slept in, but that didn't matter as there was no school, because of the floods. She got dressed and went downstairs.

Her mum and dad had gone back down to 29 River Road to inspect the flood damage with a man from the insurance company. Gran was in the kitchen.

'Morning, sleepyhead. Cup of tea?'

'Please. Where's Uncle Stanley?'

'He's down the bottom of the garden looking at his old beehive – the very first one he had. There's no bees in it. Not any more. It's been empty for years. He says he's thinking of taking it back to New Zealand with him, for old time's sake.'

Sally nodded and peered through the kitchen window down the long garden to the solitary figure mooching around beneath the apple trees.

'Have some breakfast, then it might be a good time to . . . you know,' said Gran, nodding in Uncle Stanley's direction.

Outside the air smelled fresh. It was warm and every-thing sparkled in the sunlight. Stanley Buckle sat on a wooden bench beneath the apple trees inspecting the old beehive. The hive was squarish with a little sloping roof. It was mostly white, but someone, sometime or other, had painted a large red daisy on the back. Over the years it had faded to a pale pink and had mostly flaked off, so that if you didn't know it was supposed to be a flower, you'd have had a hard time guessing.

'Gran says this was your first beehive.'

'That's right. A real "golden oldie" from the nineteen sixties.'

There was a pause while they both stared at the faded flower.

'What's it like keeping bees?'

'How do you mean?'

'Well. Aren't you afraid . . . I mean . . . don't you get stung a lot?'

'No,' laughed Stanley Buckle, 'not that often. Bees are quite particular about who they sting. You see, leaving the sting behind rips out her insides. She'll only have half an hour at the most to live. So you've got to get a bee really angry before she'll sting you.'

'You keep saying "she". Is it just the female bees that sting?'

'That's right. The workers are all females and they're the dangerous ones, the ones with the sting. The poor old drones, the males, have no sting at all. In fact, come the autumn, the workers will kill the drones to save on honey.'

'No!'

''Fraid so. There's no room for sentimentality, not in a working hive. A working hive's a business and getting rid of the drones is what you might call a "managerial decision".' And he smiled wistfully, as if remembering something, or someone, from long ago.

'Uncle Stanley?'

'Yes?'

'Are you going to the exhibition opening in London tonight?'

He sighed and hung his head.

'No. I don't think so. The roads are still flooded. It's not worth the risk. I called the Tate Gallery earlier and left a message for Neville. He'll be that busy he'll probably not even notice we're missing.'

'We?'

'Ah . . . yes. That was going to be my little surprise. I was going to ask you if you'd like to come along, as my guest.'

13

'Oh,' said Sally, feeling all happy and sad at the same time.

'I'm sorry; it would have been great fun. But floods are floods.' And he held out his hands and shrugged his shoulders.

They both looked down at the ground.

'Maybe . . .' he said, 'maybe we could do something else?'

'Like what?'

'I don't know. *You* decide.'

'Would you tell me a story?'

'A *story*?'

'Yes. The story of how you got that painting by Neville Windrush. The story about the bullet hole.'

Stanley Buckle didn't say a word, but a smile spread slowly across his face. It was the same smile Sally had noticed in the photograph album. In all those years it hadn't changed.

CHAPTER ONE

Bridge Over Troubled Waters

The summer of 1966 was what they called 'The Summer Of Love'. It was the height of 'Flower Power', 'Free Love' and 'Ban The Bomb'. The Beatles were conquering the world and the Americans were walking in space. Anything seemed possible, even in Welford, despite the fact that in 1966 more rain fell on Welford than anywhere else in Britain. The River Windrush flooded twice that year, once in April, and again in October.

I suppose this story begins on a wet Friday night sometime in April. I remember, I'd been to the pictures in Shipston with a friend called David Hutchinson. We'd seen *The Alamo*, which was a western starring John Wayne. When we came out it was dark and the rain was clattering down. We stood for ages waiting for a bus, until someone stopped and told us that there weren't any buses running because the road was flooded somewhere. We started walking; there wasn't much choice. Pretty soon we were soaked to the skin, but once you get *really* wet, it doesn't seem to matter any more. It's just that bit between being dry and then not dry that's miserable.

There used to be a bridge over the river where it ran alongside the playing fields. People'd stand on it to get a grandstand view of the football. It's gone now, they pulled it down after they built the new ring road. But that Friday night it was packed, half of Shipston had turned out to watch the Windrush in flood.

The playing fields had gone. There was a full moon and you could just make out the top bars of the goal-posts poking through the water, and it wasn't still water. It was fast-moving, roaring water that was being blown into waves by the wind. I squeezed through the crowd and pulled myself up onto the railings to get a better view.

'Careful there, Stanley. There's sausages to deliver tomorrow.'

It was Mr Righton, the butcher. He was a big, jolly man with a face the colour of minced beef. For the past six months I'd been working for him on Saturdays, doing deliveries. I had a black bicycle with a wire cage on the front for carrying. The job gave me a chance to save a bit of money, which I needed, 'cause there wasn't a fat lot about since Dad died.

'No football for a while,' he said, nodding down at where the playing fields had been.

'No,' I agreed, then nearly jumped out of my skin as a tremendous web of lightning lit up the entire bridge and everyone on it. For a second or two no-one spoke. There was a rumble of thunder, another flash, and we all stood still as statues, staring in disbelief, as the first of the white beehives sailed into view.

'Well I'll be . . .' began Mr Righton. 'It's the Spanish Armada.' And you could see what he meant. There were six of them altogether, being tossed backwards and forwards like ghostly galleons in a nightmare storm. Everyone cheered madly as one got stuck on top of a goalpost, four sank and the other sailed off into the night, never to be seen again. Then the crowd thinned out and Mr Righton gave us a lift home.

The next day, after I'd finished my deliveries, I was sweeping up the sawdust round the back of the shop when Mr Righton appeared in the doorway.

'One more delivery, but you'll not get this one on your bike. Come on, give us a hand and I'll give you a lift back home in the van. Righton's taxi service, at your service.'

We carried out the butchered pig. It was in two halves, the head was separate. We lay them in the back of the van, alongside my bike, and set off for Tappingwall Farm.

On the way we passed the playing fields. Mr Righton pulled over and rolled down his window. The noise of squawking gulls was deafening. The river had shrunk back to something more like its normal size, but the playing fields were a mess. They were covered in brown mud and pools of water and what looked like loads of silvery sweet wrappers, scattered all over. But they weren't sweet wrappers, they were fish – dead fish. It was party-time for the seagulls. Then we saw the beehives, lined up in a neat row against the wall of the boy's changing rooms.

'Looks like the Armada's dropped anchor,' said Mr Righton. 'Let's take a closer look.'

He parked the van and we walked across the sodden grass to the changing rooms.

'No name,' he said, tilting one of the hives over so that he could see the back, 'just a flower.'

One by one we tilted over the other hives. Each one had its own flower, about the size of a dinner plate, painted on the back.

'Flowers?' he muttered. 'Expect they belong to

some of them hippy-types. You know, "Flower Power", and all that nonsense.'

'I think I know where they're from,' I said.

Mr Righton raised his eyebrows, pursed his lips, and waited.

'I think they're from the Old Mill down in Welford. I don't deliver there but I cycle past on my way home and I'm sure I've seen them in the garden at the back. It's the flowers. I recognize the flowers painted on the back. Different colours for different hives.'

'Well, that solves it. They'll belong to that Windrush fellow, the artist, same name as the river. He's lived here all his life, although I expect he's wishing he lived somewhere else right now. He must have been flooded out down there. "Niagara Falls" they calls it, where the Windrush squeezes through the bottom down by the mill, and that's on a quiet day. Tell you what, let's load these hives into the back of the van and we'll drop them off on the way.'

We dropped the pig off first, then set off down the hill towards the Old Mill.

'He's an artist, is he?' I asked.

'Aye, one of those "modern" artists by all accounts. Like that Picasso fellow. The one that sticks eyes where there's meant to be a nose and a nose where there's meant to be a mouth. You know the fellow I'm on about. He's a millionaire. A genius they reckon. But if you asks me, the only thing he's a genius at is conning folks into buying his daft paintings. Personally, I likes something I can recognize – a nice bowl of fruit, or maybes a sunset.'

'What sort of things does Mr Windrush paint?'

'Haven't a clue. Don't know anyone what's been inside. Keeps himself to himself and doesn't eat much meat, that much I do know.'

We reached the bottom of the hill and skidded to a halt on the mud that covered the road. It was a battleground. Everything in the garden was flattened.

'Dear me,' muttered Mr Righton.

'That's where the beehives were,' I said, pointing towards an old pear tree that was still surrounded by water.

We climbed some stone steps and knocked on the door. There was no answer. I pressed my face up against a little window, but there was just a grey curtain of cobwebs.'

'There doesn't seem to be anybody home.'

'No,' agreed Mr Righton, 'but his car's there.' And he pointed to an old white Ford Cortina that was quite ordinary looking, except that through the front windscreen you could see, hanging from the rearview mirror, a large orange plastic lobster. Mr Righton saw it too, but didn't say anything.

'What'll we do?'

'We'll unload the hives and leave them here.

They're obviously his. He's probably out right now looking for them.'

So we did and were just getting back into the van when we heard a crash from somewhere inside the mill. We both looked up and saw a face, just for a second, at one of the upstairs windows. The face wore big black 'owl' glasses.

Mr Righton got back in the van. 'Come on. I expect he's got a lot on his mind.'

Nothing more was said. And that was the first time I saw, or *didn't* see, the famous Neville Windrush.

CHAPTER TWO

Hello, Goodbye

The following Saturday, I'd been at the butcher's shop for about an hour, scrubbing chopping blocks till my arms felt like they were made of wood. I loaded up the wire cage on the bike with the deliveries and I was wheeling it out the front when Mr Righton stopped me. He was balancing a small paper parcel at shoulder level, like a waiter carrying a tray in a posh restaurant.

'Special delivery,' he said.

'Who for?'

'Friend of yours,' he replied mysteriously. 'Mr Neville Windrush, no less. He called today. Telephoned. Apologized for not answering the door last week and ordered half a pound of ox liver. Funny that. Had him down as one of those vegetarian types. Still, it's an ill wind . . .'

'D'you want me to go there first?'

'No, you can drop it off on your way home. He wanted to thank me for rescuing his beehives. I told him it was my eagle-eyed delivery boy that deserved the thanks.'

The deliveries went smoothly and by the end of the afternoon there was just the small parcel of ox liver left in the bottom of the wire cage. I free-wheeled down the hill with my hands squeezing both brakes because of the mud. My head was full of imaginary abstract paintings and orange plastic lobsters, so by the time I arrived at the bottom I was thinking that maybe I'd just leave the liver at the top of the steps, or push it through the letter box. I wasn't sure I wanted to meet this Neville Windrush. He seemed a bit of a weirdo. But I knew Mr Righton insisted all the deliveries were handed over personally so I took a deep breath and lifted my arm to knock on the door. But before my knuckles touched the wood it swung open. I stood there with a clenched fist staring into the thick whirlpool lenses of Neville Windrush's 'owl' glasses.

He took them off and started cleaning them with the bottom of his jumper, blinking at me with pale grey eyes. His hair was a sandy coloured mop with a streak of bright orange dragged through the middle. I guessed this was paint that had rubbed off when he scratched his head, because his hands were covered in the same orange. In fact, everything he wore was splattered with paint. I kept thinking how my mum always said, 'Now be careful not to get any of that stuff on your clothes.' And that was just a little box of watercolours! This was serious paint.

'You'll be Stanley Buckle,' he said eventually.

I just nodded, noticing that I was still holding my clenched fist at shoulder height. I opened the fingers then scratched my head, self-consciously.

'Neville Windrush. I won't shake your hand.' And he held out both of his hands, palms up, so I could see all the orange paint. 'I'm in the middle of something.'

'I brought the liver.'

'I know. Come in.'

He turned round and walked back inside. I left my bike and followed him. He was quite tall, like my dad had been, only thicker set. Not really fat, more what Gran Buckle calls 'big-boned.' When he moved it was slowly and deliberately, but with a bit of a bounce that reminded me of a cartoon bear I'd seen on the telly.

He was wearing a baggy jumper, jeans and sandals. The jumper was *mostly* brown and the jeans were *mostly* blue, but there was also every other colour you could think of smeared and spattered across them.

Downstairs was one massive room with what looked like a kitchen at one end and either a bedroom or a living area, or maybe both, at the other. The walls were bare stone, just like on the outside, and high up near the ceiling were hundreds and hundreds of books, mostly art books and cookery books, all jumbled together.

In the middle of the room was a huge wooden table covered in newspapers and breakfast things and a giant blue ashtray that said something in French and was piled high with dark brown fag ends. There was a typewriter, an empty glass, and a bottle that said *Tio Pepe*. That was sherry. I knew that because there was a bottle in our corner cupboard at home. It had been there for years because Mum only ever got it out at Christmas.

'Would you like a cup of tea? Kettle's just boiled.'

'I'd best be getting home.'

'You've finished for the day then?'

'Yes,' I said, remembering the liver and handing it over.

I watched as he carefully unwrapped the parcel and slid the contents onto a battered tin plate. Then he reached into one of the kitchen drawers, removed a large pair of scissors, and began carefully snipping the purpley brown slivers into bite-sized chunks.

All the time I was thinking I should leave, but I was glued to the spot, listening to the *snip, snip*. I was half expecting him to pick it up with his orange fingers and swallow the stuff raw. Instead, he knelt down, rattled the tin plate on the floor, and in sauntered the biggest, meanest-looking ginger tom-cat I'd ever clapped eyes on.

'Meet Vincent,' he said, nodding down at the mass of ginger fur that was already chomping its way through the liver. He walked over to the sink, washed the blood off his hands, then poured a kettle of hot water into a large yellow teapot. He put the teapot down on the table and went back over to the sink to fetch two cups from a stack of dirty dishes. He looked inside them, tipped them upside down, and gave them a shake.

'Not fussy, are you?'

'No,' I said.

'Good,' he said, clunking them down on the table. 'Take milk?'

'Yes.'

He opened the fridge door and a pale green ball of lettuce rolled out onto the floor and between the legs of the table.

'Goal,' he said, leaving it where it was and reached inside for an almost empty bottle of milk. He lifted off the crumpled silver foil cap and held the bottle up to his nose.

'Smells a bit off. Shall we risk it?'

'Might as well.'

He pushed aside some of the newspapers and I sat down at the table. He sat opposite and began pouring the tea. When he added the milk it curdled and floated to the top in white lumps.

'To tell you the truth, I don't normally bother with tea once the sun's past the yardarm.' He reached across for the sherry bottle. 'I don't suppose . . .' he said, raising his eyebrows and peering over the top of the owl glasses.

'No. I'd best not. My mum lets me have a little glass at Christmas, but that's special. I don't mind the milk. Honest.' And I took a sip of tea to prove it. It was disgusting.

'Just as you like.'

He poured himself a glass of sherry then took a green-and-gold tin from his pocket. He flipped off the lid and lifted out a small rectangular packet, from which he pulled a sheet of thin paper, white on one side and dark brown on the other. He stuck this to his bottom lip and pulled out some strands of tobacco from the tin. Then he pulled the paper off his lip and held it between his finger and thumb while he arranged the tobacco in a neat row along the middle of the paper. Next he rolled the paper backwards and forwards between the first finger and thumb of each hand until it was a long dark brown tube, which he lifted back up to his mouth and ran across the tip of his tongue. Finally he snipped the loose tobacco off one end and put the fag between his lips.

'Never seen anyone roll their own before?' he asked.

'No.'

'Nothing to it. Do it with my eyes shut sometimes . . . I don't suppose you've a light?' he said, patting his pockets with his orange palms.

'No.'

'Always losing blasted matches. I've a box here *somewhere*.'

He pushed back his chair, knocking aside the now empty tin plate. The massive ginger tomcat yowled and ran out of the room.

'Ooops, never mind, he'll be back. He turned up in the garden six years ago with a swollen eye, scratches on his nose and one ear missing. Must have been a hell of a fight. Probably an Alsatian, possibly a small car.'

He'd found the matches and lit his fag. As he was doing it, he was putting the liquorice papers back in the tin and it was only afterwards that I realized he'd opened the matchbox and struck the match one-handed. He blew a cloud of smelly smoke across the table and I tried not to cough.

'I fixed his eye and nose, but the ear was gone for good. The vet wrapped a bandage round the wound.

I tried to find out if he'd a home, but no-one claimed him and he settled in the studio upstairs. He seems to like watching me paint. That's why I called him Vincent. The painting and the . . .'

'The bandage,' I interrupted.

'Good!' he said, taking a gulp of sherry. 'You know your artists then?'

'Everybody knows about Vincent Van Gogh. How he went mad and cut off his ear.'

'And all for the love of a good woman. Popped it in an envelope and posted it to her for a little keep-sake. Bit like delivering meat.'

'*Ugh!* That's disgusting.'

'Great painter, though. Didn't give a monkey's for what anyone thought. He had passion, real passion, and that's what counts. Did you know that he only ever sold two paintings in his entire life?'

'No.'

'Yep. Only two and they were for peanuts. His brother, Theo, kept him alive – bought his paints, paid his bills – and now just look at what your average Van Gogh is worth – millions! It's criminal when you think about it. You've got to be dead to be famous these days.'

He emptied the glass and poured another one. 'So, you like art?'

'I'm not any good at it.'

'That's not the same thing. You can like it without

being good at it. Same as you can enjoy watching football without being able to kick a ball.'

'I suppose what I meant is, I don't really *understand* it. Not modern art.'

'Do you like listening to music?'

'Yes.'

'Do you *understand* music? I mean, can you read a score sheet, or play several instruments?'

'No.'

'But you still enjoy it?'

'I suppose so.'

'Well, art's no different, even modern art.' And he gestured up at a painting on the wall. It was a painting of different sized red squares scattered across a pale blue background. 'You don't need to understand it. You've just got to let yourself *feel* it,' he continued.

I stared hard at the painting thinking, What's a red square feel like anyway?

'No luck, eh?' he said, scratching the back of his neck.

'What's it meant to be?'

'It's called *Red Squares On A Blue Background*.'

I nodded. There was an awkward silence. I sipped at the disgusting tea and felt his eyes staring at me from the other side of the table. He stubbed out what was left of his fag in the giant blue ashtray and stood up.

'Fetch your tea,' he said. Then he ambled over to the far end of the room where some wide wooden stairs climbed up into the shadows. I followed him, tea in hand, feeling like an explorer about to enter some undiscovered jungle. There was a strange smell that seemed to be growing stronger and stronger. It wasn't unpleasant, just different. I stopped and sniffed.

'Oil paint,' he said, glancing back over his shoulder. 'You can keep your Chanel Number Five. Linseed oil and turps, best perfume in the world.'

When I got to the top of the stairs I was standing at the end of a long dark corridor made narrow by the stacks of paintings that were leaning with their faces to the walls. They reminded me of tombstones. Neville Windrush was up ahead, he reached out and pushed open a huge white door covered with painty fingerprints. I can remember it like it happened yesterday. The end of the corridor, where he was standing, was suddenly flooded with brilliant sunlight and you could see millions of specks of dust swirling about in the air like a miniature universe of planets and stars. The smell of fresh oil paint rolled down the corridor in an invisible wave. I walked through it, through the dust, past the dead paintings, towards the light, and stepped inside.

The studio walls were dazzling white, which seemed strange at first, because there was only one

31

small window. But when you looked up it was as if there wasn't a ceiling there at all. Instead there were these huge rectangles of glass, filled with blue sky and small white clouds, moving very slowly. It was so calm and peaceful, until you looked back down. Then it was like there'd been an explosion in a paint factory.

There were crumpled paint tubes, overturned buckets, puddles of paint, fat brushes, thin brushes, dirty coffee cups, loads of empty 'Tio Pepe' bottles, painty rags. You name it, it was there somewhere, piled up on the tops of tables or just dropped on the floor.

'Watch where you put your feet. A lot of these dollops of paint are wet. Especially the orange ones.'

He walked across the floor, completely ignoring his own advice, and leaving a trail of orange footprints. I followed him as best I could.

'Have a seat,' he said, gesturing towards an ancient leather armchair, that was leaking stuffing and smeared with paint.

'It's all right, I'll stand.'

'Yes, that's probably best,' he said, looking down at the armchair as if he was seeing it for the very first time. I hid my cup of tea behind a bucket and when I looked up he'd turned round and was staring at the wall. It was only then that I noticed the painting.

It was as tall as I was, mostly orange all over,

except at the top where it was bluey green with blobs of white. The paint was that thick, that if it'd been dry you could have climbed up it. I knew he was going to ask me what I thought. I was dreading it because, to be honest, I couldn't see much difference between the painting on the wall and the paint on the floor we'd just walked across.

'This is the *new* Neville Windrush. Paintings of *passion*! No more dead squares, just hot-blooded brushstrokes. That's the way forward.'

'Why?'

'Because . . . because I say so. Because I feel like it.'

'Is it finished?' I asked.

'I think so.'

'I like it better than the coloured squares.'

'Good.'

'Has it got a name?'

'It's called *Orange Mountain Under A Green Sky*.'

I stood and stared at it for a long time, waiting for the orange to become a mountain and the green to become a sky, but it didn't click. It was that swirly green with the white blobs. There was no way it could ever be a sky, not in a million years. I started tilting my head on one side then the other, like you see owls do sometimes, and suddenly it began to make sense.

'Have you tried turning it upside down?' I asked. And then wished I hadn't.

'There's only one way up. Either it works or it doesn't.'

'Sorry.'

'No need.'

We talked for a bit longer about his paintings and my school and his bees and my job with Mr Righton, until it really was time to go. I was on my bike and ready to start pedalling uphill when he appeared at the top of the steps with a jar in each hand. One was pale gold and the other dark amber.

'I almost forgot,' he panted. 'Your reward. The last of the Old Mill honey. Heather and hawthorn. Darkness and light.'

CHAPTER THREE

The Dangling Conversation

Much to Mr Righton's amusement, the half pound of ox liver became a regular Saturday order. I told him about Neville Windrush's cat and how he'd got his name, but I don't think Mr Righton had heard of Vincent Van Gogh, because when I tried to explain about the severed ear and the bandage he gave me the same kind of look he'd given the orange plastic lobster, when he'd seen it dangling from the rearview mirror of Neville Windrush's Ford Cortina. I decided to keep quiet about seeing inside the studio. There was too much I didn't understand, including why, when I went back the following

Saturday, the big orange painting was hanging upside down on the kitchen wall.

I started spending more and more time at the studio. Every Saturday he'd have a new painting he wanted to show me. It didn't seem to matter that I didn't like them much. Half the time it just looked like he'd been standing at one end of the studio, throwing paint at the wall opposite. I didn't tell him that, but I didn't pretend to like them either and I think he respected that.

He took the trouble to introduce himself to my mum and check that it was all right for me to stop off there on Saturdays. Mum was funny. The only thing she wanted to be sure about was that he didn't have any naked ladies up there. She had this idea that all artists had naked ladies lying around their studios. Once she found out he was just a 'messy' landscape painter she was quite happy. So was I, I really looked forward to those studio visits. It felt like some sort of privilege, like being part of a secret society. It was all so different from anything at home. Apart from the mess there was the smells, and the colours, and the sounds.

Neville had a record player in the corner of his studio with a stack of old jazz records from America. They all had these fantastic names like Fats Waller, Dizzy Gillespie and Jelly Roll Morton. The music was wild. I'd never heard anything like it. It was a bit like looking at his paintings. There'd be this jumble of different instruments, this noise that was really difficult to listen to, and the harder you tried the worse it sounded. But when you stopped trying and just let the music happen you began to hear a tune that was somewhere inside the tangle of sounds. And slowly the tune grew louder and stronger until that's all there was and you could feel yourself moving with the music. That's what began to happen with the paintings, but not straightaway.

It was the beginning of October. Neville and I had been friends for nearly six months. I'd finished for the day at Mr Righton's and I was pedalling down the hill as fast as I could to the Old Mill. The wind was making my eyes water and stretching my cheeks round the back of my head. I was trying not to touch the brakes and I was going faster and faster. The sun was low down and shone through the trees so that it seemed to be flashing off and on very fast. The leaves were changing colour and out of the corners of my eyes I could see splashes of yellow and dots of orange amongst the green, but I was going that fast that by the time I looked up they'd have gone and there'd be another colour there instead. It was like watching Neville paint. I skidded to a stop and ran upstairs.

'What do you think?' asked a blue Neville.

The painting on the wall looked much like all the

others. The only difference seemed to be the colour. There was lots of blue with bits of white and lumps of red and black, but there was something else as well. Something like the tune trapped in the tangle of sounds. I stepped back a bit and slowly, the bits of white sitting on the blue became the crests of waves. The blue was the sea crashing over rocks that before had just been the lumps of red and black. It was like seeing double. There was this mess of paint, and at exactly the same time, there was this sea. So that you could almost smell the salt and hear the screeching of the gulls.

'It's the sea,' I said, smiling.

'The Pentland Firth,' said Neville.

'I'd never have guessed that much.'

'I wouldn't have expected you to. I didn't know myself until after I'd finished it.'

'How can you paint somewhere without knowing?' I asked.

'Good question. I'm not sure I've got the answer. All I know is that it was like getting your holiday photographs back twelve years later.'

'Where was it you went?'

'The Isle of Hoy, in the Orkneys. I spent a summer there, years and years ago, and I suppose it took root in my head. Some places are like that, they become part of you. So that, sooner or later, you've to go back and when you do it's like you've never been away, like looking in a mirror.'

'Are you going to go back now?'

There was a long silence. He took his fag out of his mouth and dropped it on the floor, where it stuck in a blob of blue oil paint. There was the faintest *hiss*.

'I'm not sure I want to look in that "mirror". I suppose I'm a bit scared of what I might find after all these years. The fact is, I ran away from something.'

'What?'

Neville gazed into the blue painting. Whatever the answer was, it was tangled up with too many difficult memories.

'Come on. Let's go and sit in the garden. I could use some fresh air,' he said.

The Old Mill was surrounded by trees and the air was full of dead leaves, swirling in great yellowy orange clouds. The sun had sunk behind the hill and it was beginning to grow dark. A cold breeze rustled the bare branches and the rooks were restless.

'Noisy birds,' muttered Neville. 'You get used to them though. Just like everything else. To tell you the truth, I've always had a bit of a soft spot for crows. The way they build their nests altogether, high in the treetops and fly for miles looking for food. A bit like bees.

'But the old gamekeepers seem to hate them. I'm

always finding dead crows strung up on barbed wire fences, and in the spring I've run outside more than once to stop someone blasting their nests with a shotgun. They're not empty nests either. They'll wait till there's eggs inside, or even chicks. There's no sport in it. The idea seems to be, simply to kill as many crows as quickly as possible. It's terrible . . . Why?'

'I've heard farmers say they'll peck out the eyes of a new-born lamb,' I said.

'Is that right?'

'They're predators. You can tell because their eyes are close together, set near the front of their head. They spot their meal and go for it. Birds that aren't predators, smaller birds, have eyes round the sides of their head. They're more concerned with looking over their shoulders, worrying about *becoming* a meal.

'There's lots of different types of crow. These are rooks, but there's also hooded crows, carrion crows, jackdaws, ravens, magpies and choughs. Choughs are quite rare. They've got bright red legs and beaks and live by the sea on steep cliffs. One day, when we were on holiday in Wales, me and my dad saw all seven types.'

'All at once?'

'No. But all in the same day.'

'You're a bit of an expert then.'

40

'It was my dad that got me interested. We used to go bird-spotting together.'

'"Used" to?'

'Yes . . . my dad died, when I was eight.'

'Oh,' said Neville quietly, removing his glasses and blinking his pale grey eyes, 'I didn't realize. I never thought to ask. I just assumed . . .' Then he reached down and picked up a dead twig, and after staring at it for a bit, snapped it in two. 'Right then,' he said. 'Let's make a deal. You teach me all you know about birds and I'll teach you all I know about . . . What can I teach you?'

'Bee-keeping,' I suggested.

'Bee-keeping it is then. I can see it now, *Buckle's Blossom Honey – Spread All Over Britain!* Only, I don't have any bees since the flood. Five terrific hives, but no bees. All hands lost at sea. Still, a minor detail. We'll improvise.'

'Will you be getting some more?'

'No, not just yet. I got a letter from Goldwater Fine Art this morning. They want me to have an exhibition of new paintings early next year.'

'Is that the gallery in London you told me about?'

'Yep.'

'That's good then. Isn't it?'

'It would be, but I'm still struggling. There's no way I'll be ready. Not unless . . .'

'*CAWCAWCAWCAWCAWCAWCAWCAWCAW*

*CAWCAWCAWCAWCAWCAWCAWCAWCAW
CAWCAWCAWCAWCAWCAW.*' The rooks suddenly spiralled upwards in a great black blizzard, then folded their wings and fell like rocks to the ground, recovering in the nick of time and flapping back up into the trees.

'Rain,' said Neville. 'They always do that before it rains.'

CHAPTER FOUR

Get Back

The rooks were right. The first drops of rain fell out of the darkness before I was half way up the hill. By the time I got home it was chucking it down and it hardly stopped for seven days.

The following Friday we were all sent home early from school because there were flood warnings on the radio. The River Windrush was rising fast. Everyone was dead excited, but I was worried about Neville. The river must have been creeping closer and closer to the Old Mill and I was wondering whether he'd remember to move the beehives.

When I got home there was no-one there. Mum and Rachel had gone to see Auntie Helen. They weren't coming home till six, but they'd left the key round the back in the shed.

I didn't see it at first. It was only when I came out of the shed and turned to close the door that I saw it standing in the middle of the lawn – a beehive, with a large red daisy painted on the back. I could see there was a note pinned to the side in a plastic bag, but the plastic bag had blown open in the wind and the bottom was full of watery blue ink. I reached inside and pulled out a sodden piece of paper. The rain had washed the message away, all except six words: *to look in the mirror, Neville.*

What did he mean? Why had he brought that beehive all the way up here? I was all set to jump on my bike and go and ask him when someone squeezed the clouds and the rain began falling in buckets. I ran inside, took off my wet things and got into a hot bath. Neville could wait till tomorrow – at least, that's what I thought.

On Saturday morning I woke up listening to a distant roaring coming from somewhere outside. It sounded a bit like the wind, except the wind usually blew in gusts, and this was a steady roar. I lay in bed, eliminating the possibilities – not the wind, not an engine, not a lion that had escaped from the zoo. Then it hit me – *the river*!

I threw back the covers, pulled on some clothes, ran outside and jumped on my bike. I pedalled like mad downhill in the pouring rain, but I didn't get very far. Halfway down the hill there was a police car with its blue lights flashing. It was parked across the middle of the road, stopping all the traffic. I got off my bike and walked up to one of the policemen who was trying to set up a ROAD CLOSED sign. The wind was howling, the rain was pouring and the noise of the river in the valley below was deafening.

'What's happening?' I shouted at the policeman.

'Flooding. Road's closed,' he shouted back, pointing down at the sign which had just blown over.

'What about the Old Mill?'

He shrugged his shoulders.

'There's somebody lives there. My friend, Neville Windrush.'

'Well if he's any sense he'll have got out last night while he still could.'

'Can you check?'

'Look, I've got my orders,' he said, getting irritated, 'and they don't include suicide missions to Welford Mill. Now run along home, sonny, and stop wasting valuable police time. You shouldn't be out on your bike in this kind of weather anyway.'

I turned round and left him struggling with the sign. The wind kept snatching at my bike as I pushed it back up the hill and the rain clawed at my hands, face and legs till they stung.

It was four days later before the flood water began

to go down and five or six days before anyone could get anywhere near the Old Mill. They found Neville's Cortina, complete with orange plastic lobster, half a mile away, hanging upside down in a tree. But they couldn't find Neville, or, for that matter, Vincent.

The upstairs studio was the same as always, there was even a half-finished painting on the wall and a half-empty bottle of sherry by the side of Neville's chair. But downstairs the flood had wreaked havoc. The furniture had been smashed to matchwood and all his books were ripped to shreds and scattered like giant confetti across the muddy floor. Outside, the garden was gone. His four remaining hives had gone with it and were never seen again. Even the old pear tree was uprooted and broken in two.

People were stunned. It was what they still refer to as 'The Great Flood of Sixty-Six'. Although, what was that 'great' about it was beyond me. It was a major disaster. Four people died. Two were drowned, trapped in their cars, and another two were drowned trying to rescue their pets.

The national newspapers reported the tragedy, FLOOD WATERS CLAIM FOUR LIVES IN WELFORD. ONE MAN STILL MISSING. That man was Neville. They dragged the river from here down to Shipston and back again, but they didn't find him. They found his jacket and a shoe with blue paint on, but Neville Windrush had disappeared off the face of the earth.

After a few weeks there was another headline, ARTIST STILL MISSING. And after a few more it was, FAMOUS ARTIST DROWNS IN HEROIC ATTEMPT TO SAVE CAT. All of a sudden Neville was famous. Goldwater Fine Art sent a big black van up from London and cleared out his studio. All the attention he was getting would have seemed funny, except that Neville wasn't there to share the joke. The mill was boarded up. The police investigation into his disappearance was called off. And Neville Windrush became officially 'missing, presumed dead'.

I don't know why, but I wasn't that upset, not at first. The truth was, I didn't really believe he'd drowned. After all, they hadn't found his body. And there was something else, something that was much harder to explain; I suppose you'd call it, instinct. I just knew that there was more to the story than FAMOUS ARTIST DROWNS IN HEROIC ATTEMPT TO SAVE CAT. There was something missing and it wasn't just Neville.

Where'd he gone? And why had he gone? And why didn't he come back? I kept asking myself the same questions, over and over, until winter turned into spring and spring started to turn back into summer. I tried to hide how I felt, the same way I had when Dad died. But I couldn't fool Mum. She kept me busy. She encouraged me to get my own swarm of bees and fill the empty hive that Neville had left behind. And she suggested that I put my name down for this birdwatching trip to Scotland, that our local club had organized. My friend, David Hutchinson, was going and it would 'take my mind off things'.

The trouble was, I didn't want my mind taken off things. Sometimes I'd get on my bike and pedal down to the Old Mill and just sit in the garden, like I used to with Neville. It'd be quiet. Just the sound of the river and the rooks. Then I'd hear a rustling in the nettles and I'd half expect Vincent to step out, looking for his half pound of liver. And once I heard someone banging with a hammer and I ran back up the garden thinking it was Neville trying to get back in. But it was just a man from the estate agents who'd come to put up a FOR SALE sign.

It felt like there was some sort of conspiracy. Everyone, except me, seemed to want Neville dead. The estate agents wanted the mill; the newspapers wanted his life story; the gallery in London wanted his paintings; and the police had better things to do than chase after missing persons, especially those that were missing, presumed dead.

But he wasn't. I knew he wasn't. And then, one Friday night, when I got back home from school, Mum said, 'There's something come in the post today for you. It's got a London postmark.'

'Where?'

'On the mantelpiece.'

I picked up the envelope and looked at my name,

Stanley Buckle Esq. Inside was a glossy folded card. I stared at the painting that was printed in colour on the front. It was nearly all orange, except for a line of bluey green along the bottom and it was called, *Green Sea Under an Orange Cliff*. It was the first painting I'd seen in Neville's studio. The one that had been upside down. I opened the card.

Patrick Fitzwilliam and Donald Abercromby
The Directors of Goldwater Fine Art
request the pleasure of your company
on Friday 7th July 1967 at 6pm
for the opening of a memorial exhibition of important
new paintings by the late

Neville Windrush
(1932–1966)

Mum had been reading it over my shoulder. She sat down beside me and held my hand. 'Would you like to go?' she asked quietly. 'I'm sure he'd have wanted you to be there.'

And as she said it the writing on the card began to blur.

Neville was dead.

CHAPTER FIVE

Day Tripper

We went down to London on the train. Rachel stayed with Auntie Helen. Mum wore a white cotton dress which had big navy-blue spots all over it. She had white gloves, a little navy-blue handbag and navy-blue shoes to match. She looked like a film star. I took a photograph of her standing in the back garden, just before we left.

Goldwater Mews was a little street full of big expensive cars. There were two other galleries, a shop that sold nothing but cigars, and another one that sold guns. Goldwater Fine Art was in the middle, where a line of black taxis were dropping off important-looking people.

I'd never been to a proper exhibition opening before and I don't think Mum had either. We didn't know what to expect, but neither of us was expecting what we saw through the window. It was just one big party. Everyone was standing around, laughing and talking, drinking wine and nibbling at things on sticks. The older people were mostly dressed in suits, and the younger ones were all wearing the latest fashions. No-one was looking at the paintings.

'Oh, dear,' said Mum opening her handbag and taking out the invitation card. 'I wasn't expecting so many people.'

Inside there was a lot of laughing and '*yoo-hoo*'-ing and '*daaarling*'s and everyone seemed to be kissing each other, not just once, but twice – once on each cheek. I saw two people that I recognized from the telly and a whole lot of others looking as though they expected to be recognized any minute. A waiter gave Mum a glass of champagne and me a glass of orange juice.

Standing in a corner were two men who I guessed were the directors of the gallery. One was very tall with a sharp bony face. He was pointing at different paintings and waving his arms about. The other one was short with black curly hair and fat red cheeks. He kept his hands in his pockets and only brought them out to scratch the back of his neck.

Lots of people were coming up to them and shaking

their hands as if these two had painted the paintings and not Neville. 'Quite so,' I heard the tall one say, 'a *devastating* blow to the art world. This memorial exhibition was actually Donald's idea. In the circumstances, it was the least we could do.'

'There's thingy from the telly,' said Mum, sounding most impressed. 'I'd got no idea your Neville was this famous.'

'He wasn't,' I heard myself say.

'Canapé?' asked a waitress, holding a tray of nibblies.

'Look at these!' said Mum. 'I shouldn't really. Oh, well, perhaps just the one. One of those little square ones. Thank you so much.'

I took a small triangle of something fishy, but I didn't feel hungry.

'You can't see the paintings for people,' said Mum. 'But I do think we ought to make an effort.'

'Yes,' I said. And we manoeuvred our way through the crowds to the nearest wall, until we were standing in front of *Green Sea Under An Orange Cliff*.

'Is that the painting on the invitation card?' asked Mum.

'Yes. What do you think?'

'They're not really my sort of thing.'

'You need to see it from further away, but there's not much chance of that.'

'No,' said Mum, looking over her shoulder at a

woman who was laughing hysterically because she'd just dropped a prawn puff pastry nibbly into someone's glass of red wine.

'What's that red dot mean?' asked Mum, pointing to the label underneath the painting.

'I think it means that it's sold.'

'Look,' said Mum. 'They've all got those little red dots.'

And when I looked around she was right. I stepped across and read the label nearest us, *Green Sea Under An Orange Cliff, oil on canvas, 1966, £10,000.* TEN THOUSAND POUNDS! I couldn't believe it. Neville had told me that the most he'd ever sold a painting for was two and a half thousand pounds. That seemed like a lot, but *ten* . . .

'Blimey,' I said to myself.

'Pardon, dear?'

'I think I need to go to the loo.'

I left Mum squinting at another painting through an empty champagne glass and I squeezed through the crowd, past the different paintings, most of which I remembered from the studio. On the way I glanced at the prices, £10,000; £8,000; £12,000. And they *all* had red dots on their labels.

The waitress said the toilets were downstairs. I went to the loo, washed my hands and walked back to the foot of the stairs, but before I'd started to climb back up something stopped me. It was *that* smell –

the smell of fresh oil paint. It was like being back in Neville's studio.

I looked around. There was a long corridor and on either side were wooden racks that went from the floor up to the ceiling. The racks were crammed with paintings, big ones on the left and smaller ones on the right. It was dark and I couldn't really see that much, but at the very end of the corridor there was a faint red glow. Slowly, I walked towards it, glancing every now and then into the racks, where I'd catch a glimpse of a splash of colour, or a painted eye, staring out from the shadows. It was spooky. I kept expecting a real arm to reach out any second and grab me by the shoulder. I looked behind me, but there was nobody there, so I carried on. The smell of fresh oil paint was getting stronger all the time.

At the end of the corridor I came to a small room with a glass-topped desk and two leather armchairs. The red glow was coming from a burglar alarm fitted to the wall above the light switch. I clicked the light switch on. There was a large, wooden crate standing in the corner. It was covered in labels that said THIS WAY UP and HANDLE WITH CARE! and across the middle someone had stencilled the words STROMNESS TO LONDON in big black letters.

On the opposite wall were two of Neville's paintings that I hadn't seen before. There weren't any labels, but I didn't need a label to know they were by

Neville. No-one else threw paint on canvas like that!

They were both paintings of the same thing, a big column of red rock, surrounded by sea and sky. Looking at them, I felt like I was somewhere high up, soaring like a seagull. They were really good. Better than anything upstairs. It's hard to say exactly why, except they had a kind of 'energy', like they were alive almost, and that made you want to touch them. I couldn't resist. I stretched out a finger and touched the nearest painting. It was wet! But that wasn't possible. These paintings had to be at least ten months old. And that was plenty of time for even the thickest paint to dry.

I was still staring at the paintings when I heard footsteps and voices at the end of the corridor. Without thinking, I dived behind the large wooden crate that was standing just out from the other wall and crouched down on the floor. The footsteps and voices grew louder and closer.

'When did they arrive?'

'This morning. I couldn't wait, I unpacked two, the others are still in their crates.'

'You left the light on.'

'I'm sure I didn't.'

'So how many altogether?'

'Thirty-three.'

'Thirty-three! My, my. He *has* been a busy boy.'

There was silence for a bit and then the sound of a

drawer being pulled open and papers being shuffled about.

'You do realize that his prices have more than quadrupled since his "death". If we're clever about it, we could be looking at almost a million pounds.'

'There's only one small problem.'

'Yes?'

'What happens when the novelty of this little prank wears off and he decides he wants to return to the land of the living?'

'My dear Donald, the fact of the matter is, Neville Windrush is worth a lot more dead than he is alive . . . a *lot* more. We simply can't afford to let him spoil things.'

'What are you suggesting?'

'I'm suggesting a *permanent* solution. In Italy they call it "taking out a contract" on someone.'

'You mean, have him killed?'

'To put it crudely, yes, but I much prefer to think of it as simply good business practice. That's why I like the word "contract", it's all very businesslike.'

'But it's still murder.'

'Such an ugly, emotional word, Donald. Try to think of it more creatively. I shall hire a professional – the best there is. They won't be cheap, but they will be reliable.'

'So it's all settled.'

'Simply a matter of payment. Half now. And half

when Windrush is . . . well, shall we say, half when the job's done.'

'I don't know,' sighed Donald Abercromby. 'It's one thing having him "missing, presumed dead", but it's quite another having him a corpse. Corpses have a nasty habit of causing trouble. The police are bound to be suspicious if he suddenly materializes, hundreds of miles away, with a bullet in his head.'

'My dear Donald, there are ways and means of disposing of unwanted bodies. But even if Neville Windrush is strangled outside Stromness police station in broad daylight, you and I will still be in the clear. Apart from that one visit, when I was extremely careful to disguise my identity, we have had no contact with him since his timely disappearance last year, none whatsoever. No letters. No telephone calls. No written receipts. Nothing. Not even a cheque. Everything was paid for with cash. If we're asked about all these new paintings, we simply say they're not new paintings. They were painted in his studio at Welford before the flood and that the gallery bought them for cash, because that's what Neville wanted. *We simply pretend.*'

'I don't know. I still don't like it,' muttered Donald Abercromby.

'I'm not asking you to *like* it,' said Patrick Fitzwilliam, irritably. 'I'm merely asking you to consider the facts. An average Windrush is now worth £10,000 and they're selling like hot cakes. With this new shipment and the work upstairs the gallery "owns" at least fifty and that's not including all the earlier paintings we removed from his studio. The price has shot up because people think he's dead. If they suddenly discover that he is, in fact, alive and well, then the bubble bursts. But we're not going to let it burst. We're going to keep our heads and line our pockets. Because, if you'll pardon the expression, we stand to make a killing. Now, let's get back upstairs and be nice to the rabble.'

For ages I didn't dare move. I stayed crouched behind the crate, gripping my knees with my hands. I wanted to be dead sure they'd gone. I waited for what seemed like hours, but was probably just minutes, then I ran back down the corridor and up the stairs.

'There you are,' said Mum. 'I was just about to come and see what had happened to you. Are you all right?'

'Yes, thanks. I'm fine.'

'I was just having a most interesting conversation with that nice man over there,' said Mum, waving coyly.

I looked across the room and saw a tall thin man pointing a camera in our direction. There was a flash. He lowered it and waved. It was Patrick Fitzwilliam.

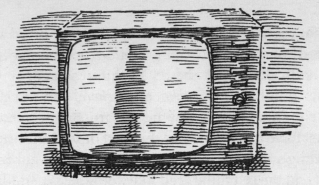

CHAPTER SIX

Wouldn't it be Nice?

I sat on the train with my face pressed against the window. It was dark outside and the black silhouettes of bushes and trees were rushing past. When I tilted my head sideways, it looked like they were falling out of the sky. There were reflections too, people's faces from inside the train, laughing and talking. It felt like the whole world was turning upside down and I was the only person that knew.

Part of me wanted to tell Mum, but the other part needed time to think. Besides, Mum was looking so happy. It was the first time she'd been out like that since my dad died and telling her what I'd heard would have spoilt things.

That night I couldn't get to sleep. I felt scared and excited, all at the same time. Excited, because Neville was still alive, and scared because someone was going to kill him. But *who*, and *where*, and *when*? It was a nightmare, a living nightmare. But eventually I must have drifted off and the next day, in the bright morning sunshine, it all felt like a dream. I was dead tired and the last thing I felt like doing, was pedalling round Shipston delivering parcels of meat.

Mum was in the kitchen, stuffing dirty clothes into the washing machine with one hand and holding the telephone to her ear, with the other. She was telling Auntie Helen what a great time she'd had in London. About the gallery, and the champagne, and the famous people off the telly. She was full of it. I knew I couldn't tell her. She'd think I'd imagined the whole thing. And I was beginning to wonder myself. Was it possible? Could I have imagined hearing that conversation downstairs in the gallery? Could they have been talking about something else? Then Mum put the phone down and held up a pair of light grey trousers, the ones I'd been wearing last night.

'How on earth do you manage it, Stanley? You hardly eat a thing all day and you still end up with tomato sauce on your new trousers.'

Then I knew that I hadn't imagined anything. It wasn't tomato sauce. It was red oil paint.

I went to get my bike from the shed. It was a perfect summer's day with a cloudless blue sky and the faintest of breezes that felt like someone breathing on your skin. It was the kind of day people went around smiling and laughing and waving to each other across the street, not the kind of day you thought about hired killers disposing of bodies.

I wheeled my bike over to Neville's beehive. I still called it Neville's, even though he must have meant me to keep it. Next door had a forest of lavender bushes that were in flower and the bees were doing overtime. I stood for a bit watching them flying back with their knees covered in pollen, doing their little dance at the entrance to the hive to tell the others exactly where they'd got it from.

'Where's Neville?' I heard myself asking. 'Where's he gone?'

I bent down and put my ear next to the hive, listening to the quiet steady buzzing that was coming from deep inside, and I remembered Neville saying that, when bees were quiet, they were happy.

Delivering the meat took my mind off things, except when I cycled past the police station. I stopped outside and thought about going in, but I could just imagine what they'd have said, 'Mr Windrush? Back from the dead then, is he? And what's this you're saying . . . these respectable art dealers are hiring a "hitman" to bump him off? Now why don't you just run along home, sonny, and stop wasting valuable police time.'

It was no use. I hadn't a shred of evidence. No-one was going to take me seriously. I knew I'd have to try and find Neville on my own and warn him before it was too late. At least that way he'd stand a chance. But how was I going to do that when I didn't even know where he was? It seemed hopeless, like trying to do a jigsaw with half the pieces missing.

'Stanley!' shouted Mum, when I got home. 'Come and look at this.' She was in the front room, standing in front of the telly. 'The things that some people do for pleasure!' she said, shaking her head.

And there, in black and white, was this man with a crash helmet on, dangling from the end of a rope, with a fag in his mouth. It was Joe Brown, the famous rock climber.

'What's this?'

'It's live television.'

'Live of what?'

'The Old Man of Hoy. It's this big sea stack thing, somewhere in the north of Scotland. They're climbing it for television.'

A shiver went up my spine. It was that word, 'Hoy'. I remembered Neville saying that's where he'd been on his holidays, years ago. My eyes were glued to the screen. The picture changed and it was the top of a cliff, with the television commentator being blown about in the wind. He said something about, 'This historic first BBC broadcast live from the Orkneys.' Then lots of crackling noises. Then, 'The notoriously difficult chimney crack on the second pitch.' And then the camera swung round – and there it was! The same column of rock. The same as I'd seen painted on the canvases, downstairs in the gallery. The ones that were still wet.

'It's been off and on all day,' said Mum. 'I think they're all mad. But that place looked nice, where they're all staying. What was it called? Strom, something.'

'Stromness,' I muttered.

'That's it. We'll have to go there one day.'

STROMNESS TO LONDON – the directions that had been stencilled across the front of the wooden crate, the one I'd hidden behind. It all added up: the wet paintings, the crate, the note Neville had left pinned to the beehive, the one the rain had almost washed away, apart from the words 'to look in the mirror'. Now I understood. He was talking about going back to Hoy. I'd found the missing pieces and the jigsaw was starting to make sense.

'Oh, and by the way, David Hutchinson called round earlier. He wants to know if you're still interested in this bird-watching trip to the Cairngorms. It's only two weeks away and you're going to have to say "yes" or "no".'

'I'd forgotten.'

'Well, David hasn't. He said there were only two places left. I was planning on going to stay with Auntie Helen around about then, so that'd work out nicely. It's just what you need, a bit of an adventure.'

CHAPTER SEVEN

Suspicious Minds

'Are y'coming then?' asked David. 'There's all sorts up there we haven't got down here. Peter Watson went last year. He got more ticks in his book than anyone else. He said he saw a peregrine falcon kill a pigeon in mid-air. It just came out of nowhere and hit the pigeon from behind. There was loads of feathers, then the pigeon started falling, but before it hit the ground the peregrine falcon had looped the loop and caught the dead pigeon in its claws. There's golden eagles too and ospreys that catch salmon straight out of the lakes. Imagine that – seeing an osprey fly off with a massive salmon in its claws. And if we're really lucky we might see a capercaillie. Peter

Watson saw one. He said they're bigger than Christmas turkeys and taste of pine cones, 'cause that's what they eat. *He* hasn't eaten one though. He just read that somewhere.'

'Sounds great.'

'Great? It sounds *fantastic*. You're coming, aren't you.'

'Yes . . . and no.'

'Yes and no? What kind of answer's that? Is y'mum stopping you?'

'No. She thinks it's a great idea. She's all for it.'

'Well?'

'If I tell you, you've got to promise not to breathe a word to anyone.'

'Sounds serious,' said David.

'It is.'

'Go on then. Cross my heart and hope to die.'

'I'm not going on the Cairngorms trip.'

'Is that it?'

'But I want everyone else to think that I am,' I added.

'Like who?' asked David.

'Like my mum. Especially my mum. She's got to think I'm up in the Cairngorms with you.'

'Why? Where'll you be?'

'Remember Neville Windrush?'

'You mean the famous artist – the one that drowned in the river, last year.'

'That's him.'

'What about him?'

'He's not dead. He's alive.'

'How do y'know?'

'He left a note, pinned to that beehive he gave me. It was all smudged with the rain and I couldn't read it at first. There was only a few words, and they didn't make sense. But now they do and I know where he is.'

'Where's that?'

I hesitated for a moment. I wasn't sure how much I wanted David to know. I had a feeling that if I told him about hearing the gallery directors plotting to have Neville killed, he'd think I was making it all up. He wouldn't take me seriously.

'The Orkneys.'

'Where?'

'They're these islands off the tip of Scotland. They're miles from anywhere.'

'What's he doing up there?'

'He's hiding.'

'Who from?'

'I don't know. But I've promised that I'll go and see him.'

'And you don't want your mum to find out?' said David.

'That's right.'

'Sounds a bit fishy t'me.'

'There's more. Neville's in danger. I can't explain. You've got to help me. *Please.*'

David looked at me long and hard.

'How?'

'The only person my mum knows in the bird-watching club is you. If you see her and she asks about the trip, just act normal, like I'm going. She won't be coming to see me off and she won't be expecting any phone calls. So once you've gone, I'll have seven whole days to sort out Neville.'

David lifted the lid off an old biscuit tin and took out his collection of postcards. They were all of birds. He spread them out on the table and picked out one of a peregrine falcon and another of a golden eagle.

'Here. Write a message to your mum on these. Tell her what a great time you're having in the Cairngorms. I'll post them while I'm there.'

The bus that was taking the bird-watching club to the Cairngorms left at six p.m. on Friday, 21 July. That was twelve whole days away: two hundred and eighty-eight hours; seventeen thousand, two hundred and eighty minutes; or, one million, thirty-six thousand, eight hundred seconds. I know because I counted most of them.

It was like someone had poured glue in the clock. I was walking around Welford, pretending everything was normal, but in my mind I'd already left.

People would talk to me and I wouldn't hear what they were saying. All I could think about was that I'd be too late. It didn't matter what I was doing, riding my bike, eating chips, watching telly, brushing my teeth, I kept seeing this faceless person walking up a narrow path to a little house on Hoy. They'd be carrying a gun. And inside the house, with his feet up on the sofa, listening to Jelly Roll Morton, was Neville. Totally oblivious.

Then there was the guilt. I hated keeping things from my mum and it was awful having to tell her lies, even 'white lies'. The guilt grew worse and worse and got harder and harder to hide. Like a cut that gets infected and turns poisonous, swelling up so that you can't bear to touch it. And you can't understand why everyone doesn't realize what you're feeling. But they don't. Because, if you're doing a good job lying, you're on your own.

By the time Friday the twenty-first came round I was almost ready to spill the beans. I desperately wanted to tell Mum everything and then ask if I could go anyway. Except I knew what she'd have said. You didn't need to be the 'Brain of Britain' to work that one out.

David came round for me at five o'clock. I had my rucksack packed and ready. I left Mum at the front door. We'd agreed that I didn't want waving off. Then David and I walked to the end of the road.

'See y' then.'

'See you,' I said, starting to feel really nervous.

'You're not getting cold feet, are you?'

'No,' I said, trying to sound braver than I felt.

'Good luck then.'

'Thanks.'

David turned left to walk to the bus station and I turned right.

'Stan!' he shouted. 'There's puffins on Orkney.'

CHAPTER EIGHT

Mrs Robinson

Two hours later I was in London, standing underneath the departures timetable at King's Cross. I'd booked a bed for myself on the overnight sleeper to Inverness. I looked along the list of destinations: Newcastle, Glasgow, Edinburgh, Aberdeen, and, yes, *Inverness, platform five, departing 21.30 hours. The rear six carriages offer sleeping accommodation.* I checked my watch. It was seven thirty.

It wasn't that long ago that I'd stood in almost exactly the same spot with my mum, but now it all felt completely different. I was in charge. I was making things happen. Being alone wasn't scary any more, because I was *doing* something. It was the not doing anything that had been scary. I'd made my mind up to find Neville and nothing was going to stop me.

I walked through a sea of pigeons that were pecking at some popcorn someone had spilt. One or two flapped their wings and flew up, but most of them just kept pecking. I stopped at a newspaper kiosk. All the newspapers had the same picture on the front. It was a photograph of an American astronaut, wearing a white padded spacesuit, floating in space. You couldn't see his face, just the reflection of a spaceship. The headline was something like STEPPING OUT INTO THE GREAT UNKNOWN.

The glass doors of the station café swung closed and the clanking of the trains turned into the clatter of teacups. Inside it was packed. Everyone else seemed to have had the same idea – to sit down and have a cup of tea. I grabbed a plastic tray and joined the end of the queue, shuffling forwards, happy to kill a bit of time.

'Cup of tea, dear?' asked the lady behind the counter.

'Yes, please. And a ham sandwich.'

I was hungry.

'There you are then. There's sugar for the tea and mustard for the ham on the table. That'll be . . .'

But I didn't hear her, because I was busy rooting in my rucksack, looking for my money. For some daft reason I hadn't packed it near the top, where I could have got to it easily. Instead it was stuffed down the side somewhere, together with my train ticket and a photograph of me and Neville that was taken in his garden last summer. I found the ticket and the photograph and put them down on my tray, while I searched for the money.

'I'm sorry,' I said. 'I've got it somewhere.'

'Don't worry, dear. No rush. Take your time.'

'Leave that where it is,' said this voice behind me. 'This is for two teas and two ham sandwiches.'

I looked up and saw an elderly lady handing a five-pound note over the counter. She looked down at me and smiled.

'Thanks,' I said. 'I'll pay you back in a minute. Soon as I've found it.'

'Just as you like. Shall we sit down?'

She was only a little bit taller than me, but almost the same across. Not really fat, more stocky. What my mum would have called 'matronly', but other people might have called 'built like a barrel'. She was wrapped up in a heavy grey overcoat, fastened round the middle with a belt and carried an army surplus canvas bag in one hand and a small battered leather case, that looked like it held binoculars, slung over her shoulder. Perched on her head was a black beret, with silvery curls bubbling out from underneath. The only splash of colour was a biggish red scarf she wore draped over her shoulders. There were black-and-white scottie dogs walking along the edge of it. Black ones down the left and white ones up the right.

There was nothing that unusual about her. Except her eyes. Instead of the iris being all one colour, like blue, or grey, or brown, hers were the palest blue on the top half and the darkest brown on the bottom. So that, even when she was staring straight at you, it looked like she was looking down.

'They're most unusual, aren't they?' she said, smiling.

'Pardon?'

'My eyes. People seldom look me in the face for long. They usually end up staring at the floor. Because that's what they think I'm doing.'

'I'm sorry. I didn't mean to be rude,' I said, staring down at the floor.

'No offence taken, young man. It's Stanley, isn't it? I sneaked a look at the label tied to your rucksack, while we were standing in the queue.'

'Stanley Buckle,' I said.

'And I'm Elsie,' she said, picking up a little pot of jam from the table and staring at the label. 'Elsie Robinson, like the jam, Robinson's Strawberry Jam.' Then she plonked the jar of jam back down on the table top and picked up a jar of mustard. She pulled apart her sandwich, stuck a knife into the jar and spread a thick layer of bright yellow, burning hot mustard all over the ham until there wasn't a trace of pink to be seen.

'Shall I do yours?' she asked, looking up, but still looking like she was looking down.

'Er . . . no, no thanks, I'm not that keen on mustard.'

'Sugar?' she asked, lifting my cup off the tray.

'No, thanks.'

'Sweet enough. I'm afraid I usually take four or five.'

She started to sugar her tea and when she lifted mine up it slopped a bit on the tray. 'Oh, how clumsy of me,' she said, putting down the cup and picking up my train ticket and photograph. 'No harm done,' she said, wiping off the few splashes of tea that had fallen on them. Then she handed back the ticket, but kept the photograph.

'Your father?' she asked.

'No. Just a friend,' I said, passing across the money I owed her.

'That's nice,' she said, putting the photograph back down and picking up the money. 'Are you travelling alone?'

'Yes.'

'Far?'

'The Orkneys,' I said.

'The Orkneys! Well, what a coincidence. I go bird-watching there every summer. In fact . . . ,' and she patted her binocular case, 'that's precisely where I'm off to in, let me see . . .' and she checked her watch, 'just over one hour's time.'

'The sleeper to Inverness?'

'Yes. Then to Thurso. Then a short bus ride to Scrabster. And finally, the ferry to Stromness. What's your reservation number?' she asked excitedly.

'E23.'

'Mine's G14. Just two carriages down. Fancy that! We're almost neighbours!'

By the time I'd finished my tea Elsie Robinson knew everything there was to know about the Buckle family history. It was hard to get a word in edgeways. I kept trying to ask her about bird-watching on Orkney. I'd say something like, 'Are there many puffins on Orkney?' and she'd say, 'Yes. Now do tell me more about the flood.' So, in the end, I gave up. She didn't seem that interested in birds. Not until we stepped outside and she saw the pigeon with the broken wing.

'Oh! Look! The poor darling. I can't bear it. I can't bear to see little creatures suffer like that. They're so helpless.'

She put her canvas bag down on the ground and shooed away the other pigeons that were round it. Then, ever so slowly and gently, she knelt down and picked it up, cradling it in one arm and stroking the back of its neck with the index finger of her other hand.

'There, there. Don't worry. Don't be frightened,' she cooed.

The wide round eyes of the pigeon seemed to be staring in horror. It was on its last legs.

'What are we going to do with you?' she asked the pigeon. 'We can't take you on the train. We'll have to find someone here to look after you. Excuse me! Porter! Would you be kind enough to take this poor bird to the Station Master's office and ask him if he'll call a vet? It's got a broken wing. Here's five pounds. That ought to cover it.'

'For five quid y'can have a new 'un, missus,' laughed the porter.

'I don't want a new one,' said Elsie Robinson, in a deep deliberate voice that wiped the smile from the porter's face. 'I want this one to receive proper care and attention. Do we understand each other?'

'Er, yes. Right you are, ma'am. I'll deal with it straightaway.'

The porter pocketed the five-pound note and walked off with the pigeon held in both hands at arm's length. I could tell he thought Elsie Robinson was completely batty and I didn't fancy the pigeon's chances, not once he was round the corner and out of sight.

'Do be careful with it!' shouted Elsie.

But he didn't look back.

'It'll be all right,' I said hopefully.

'Fingers crossed,' said Elsie, and there were tears in her eyes.

Ten minutes later I was on the train. Compartment 20–24 was empty. I pulled down the blinds, let my rucksack drop to the floor, and sunk down onto the bottom bunk. Five minutes later I was fast asleep. I don't even remember the train leaving the station, but I do remember having a dream.

I dreamt I was on a train. But the train wasn't on the ground. It was hurtling through space at a thousand miles an hour. For some reason I had to get from one carriage to another, but the only way of doing this was to climb outside.

There was a white padded spacesuit, hanging up in my compartment, so I put it on. I pulled down the window and floated outside. Everything was black. I was crawling along the roof of the carriage when somebody below me stuck their head out of a window. It was Elsie Robinson. She was shouting something. It sounded like, 'You must jump. The train is going to crash into the sun. Don't look down!' But the more I tried not to, the more I had to look down. And when I did I saw this huge yellow jar of mustard. The lid was off and you could feel the heat coming up. The train was getting closer and closer. And the circle of yellow mustard was getting bigger and bigger. I tried to jump, but I couldn't move. I'd broken my leg and it was getting hotter and hotter and hotter . . .

CHAPTER NINE

I am the Walrus

I woke up covered in sweat. The compartment was like an oven. I couldn't breathe. There was a thin line of sunlight, like white hot metal, glowing round the edge of the window blind. I jumped out of bed, pulled up the blind, and pulled down the window. The place was suddenly full of light, and noise, and gallons of fresh air that smelled cool and sweet and spun round and round the compartment, blowing that stupid dream out the window.

I pushed the window back up and the whirlwind of noise dropped to a steady *clickety-click, clickety-click, clickety-click*. Squinting outside, I saw that we'd left the cities behind. There weren't even any fences.

Just mile after mile of empty rolling hills that were turning purple with heather blossom.

I pulled up all the other blinds then checked my watch. It was nine o'clock and I was starving.

The dining car was four carriages down. It looked like they'd finished serving, but I noticed someone waving to me. It was Elsie Robinson. She was sitting at a table by herself.

'I kept you a place, Stanley,' she said. 'But, to be perfectly honest, I was beginning to think you'd jumped off the train at Newcastle. I asked the guard to check E23, and he said he thought you were still asleep because the blinds were down.'

'I slept in.'

'You don't mind me calling you Stanley, do you? You must call me Elsie. After all, we're fellow explorers. Do have some orange juice, it keeps the scurvy at bay.'

'Thanks.'

'I expect you're ravenous.'

'Yes. I am.'

'Me too. At least, I was. I always find that setting off on an expedition sharpens the appetite. Do order, I've had mine already – a brace of boiled kippers, followed by kidneys on toast, with lashing of grapefruit marmalade. I told the waiter to expect one more.'

I felt sick, but it passed. The waiter came and I

ordered bacon and beans. Elsie sat back and looked out of the window.

'I do love Scotland, don't you?' she sighed, clapping her hands together.

I thought about the question. 'It's emptier . . . and more purple, than I'd imagined.'

'Ah, yes, the heather,' she said, fixing me with her downward-looking stare. 'There's plenty of that. And emptiness. But that's all part of its charm, don't you think? You can walk for miles and miles, and not set eyes on another living soul. In fact, you could disappear altogether and no-one would be the wiser.'

'Bacon and beans, sir.' It was the waiter.

'You tuck in,' said Elsie. 'I'm off to powder my nose.'

I watched her go, squeezing between the seats with her binocular case still slung over her shoulder. She was what Mum would have called 'different', but in a nice way. I noticed someone else was watching her too. A man sitting across the aisle, lowered the newspaper he was reading. He had curly black hair and dark brown eyes and his top lip was hidden under a huge droopy walrus moustache that was starting to turn grey. You couldn't tell whether he was smiling or scowling. He saw me looking, folded the newspaper, tucked it under his arm, stood up and left. It was then that I saw his right hand was missing and in its place was a metal claw.

'Inverness in twenty minutes,' said Elsie cheerfully, when she returned. 'Time to get our things together. We'll be changing trains for Thurso, that's the end of the line. If I don't see you before, we're bound to bump into each other on the ferry.'

'I'll keep my eyes open.'

'*Do!*' she insisted, gathering up her scarf and overcoat.

I sat alone for a bit then paid the waiter and walked back to my compartment. All the corridors were blocked with people and by the time I reached E20–24 it was twenty-five past ten. I was just about to slide open the door when it slid open for me and out stepped the man with the walrus moustache.

'*Scusi*. Wrong compartment.'

The sky had clouded over and it was starting to rain. The train for Thurso left at eleven o'clock from platform three. Everyone must have piled into the first few carriages because the last carriage seemed completely empty. I opened the door, climbed on board and shut it behind me. Then I walked to the very end and slid open the door of the very last compartment. It was empty. I closed the door and sat down, leaning my forehead against the cold glass of the window, watching the grey drizzle wet the grey gravel and the brown iron tracks. The door slid open.

'*Buongiorno* . . . I mean, good morning.' It was 'the walrus' again.

'May I?' he said, gesturing to the seat opposite me.

I tried to say something, but nothing came out.

'You are expecting someone else. Yes?'

'No,' I said.

He put a small leather case on the luggage rack then sat down.

'You are travelling alone perhaps?'

'Yes,' I said, and straightaway wished I hadn't.

'So the lady I saw you with in the dining car, the lady with the black hat. She is not your companion?'

'Sort of. We met at the station. She'll probably be along any minute.'

'Ah. *Si*. You both go to the islands of Orkney.'

'Yes.'

'Me also.'

There was a loud *clunk*, and the train lurched forward. I sat back and watched Inverness disappear, remembering what Elsie had said about Scotland being the kind of place where 'you could disappear altogether and no-one would be the wiser.'

The walrus put his left hand inside his jacket pocket and pulled out a green apple. He shined it on the lapel of his jacket and placed it carefully on the seat beside him. He put his left hand back inside his jacket and pulled out a large penknife with a white bone handle. He flicked a safety catch and a long silver blade flashed open.

Then he lifted his right arm and transferred the knife to the metal claw, which closed around it. He tested the edge of the blade with his left thumb, then picked up the apple and began to peel it, turning the apple in his left hand and holding the knife, almost motionless, in the metal claw. The peel spiralled down to the floor like a long green snake. He knew I was watching him.

'Sometimes I think it would be easier to have simply a blade and not a claw. But then, there are times when I have need of a claw and not a blade.'

I just nodded.

'You have family in Orkney?'

'Just a friend.'

'You like some apple?'

'No thanks,' I said, 'What about you?'

'*Scusi?*'

'Are you on holiday?'

'Me, no,' he laughed. 'My visit is strictly business. I do not much like Scotland. Too empty. Too wet. And the coffee! It is terrible. When my business is finished I will return to Italy as quickly as possible. And now, I think I will . . . how do you say? . . . stretch my legs.'

He stood up and held out his left hand.

'Francesco Allegretto.'

'Stanley Buckle,' I said.

'Stan . . . leeee, an interesting name. I have not heard it before now.' He lifted down his small leather case and slid open the compartment door. 'In Italy we say, a man cannot choose his name, but a wise man chooses his friends carefully. *Arrivederci*, Stanley Buckle.'

The compartment door slid shut and I just sat there, barely moving, staring at the lifeless green 'snake', lying on the dusty floor. It was all falling into place. I could hear the voice of Patrick Fitzwilliam, *'In Italy they call it "taking out a contract" . . . It's all very businesslike.'*

I was scared stiff but at the same time I was dead excited, because this meant Neville was still alive. I suppose I'd half convinced myself that I'd be too late, that the hit-man, whoever he was, would have beaten me to it. After all, it'd been two whole weeks since I'd heard the directors plotting downstairs in the gallery basement, but I guess there wasn't any mad rush for them. And now, here I was, travelling to Orkney at *exactly* the same time, on *exactly* the same train, as the real hit-man.

I looked out of the window. The sky was a pale watery blue and the hills had shrunk into the dark brown bogs of Caithness. Pale blue on top, dark brown below, like Elsie Robinson's eyes.

CHAPTER TEN

Reach Out, I'll Be There

The ferry was called the *St Ola*. A line of cars and lorries trickled down a steel ramp that led deep inside its hold. They looked like a shoal of tiny fish being swallowed in slow motion by a massive whale. Most of the foot passengers were already on board. I hung back, I didn't want to be brushing shoulders with Francesco Allegretto if I could possibly help it. I figured the less he saw of me the better.

Inside it was more like a hotel than a boat. There were carpets, and shops, and cafés and messages on the tannoy system about cars and lost children and meals being served. But then it started moving and you could feel the floor begin to sway. It was

86

like trying to dance with someone you couldn't see. I bought a bar of chocolate and a can of Coke from the shop and climbed some more stairs to the Observation Deck, all the time looking out for Francesco Allegretto, but I couldn't see him anywhere.

There were doors leading outside, where you could sit on red plastic seats, but nearly everybody was inside because it had started raining again, that fine wet rain that doesn't come in drops but seems to be everywhere at once, the kind that Scotland seems to specialize in. I'd just sat down when I heard someone in the café complaining about his coffee. I quickly pulled a waterproof out of my rucksack, pushed the door open and stepped outside.

The wind slammed against me. I took a step back, lowered my head, and pushed forward to the railings. Huge grey waves rose and fell, *whooshing* and crashing against the sides of the boat, exploding into clouds of white foam, over and over. The door behind me swung open again and I turned round half expecting the walrus, but a lady stepped out. She had long red hair that was blowing about in the wind like the flames of a bonfire, and bright green eyes. She came over and stood beside me.

'Are you not afraid of being blown away?' she asked, in a lovely soft Orkney accent.

I shook my head.

'A bit seasick maybes?'

'No. I'm fine. Just came out for a bit of fresh air.'

'Aye, well there's plenty of that out here. Bit too much for me. I'll be leaving you to it.'

She smiled and went back inside.

I staggered round to the back of the boat, where the wind wasn't too bad and found a dryish seat. A white seagull came to keep me company. It was a fulmar, gliding alongside the boat, motionless, like it was hanging from some invisible thread. It couldn't have been more than three feet away. I started thinking about David, wondering how many new ticks he had in his bird book. I stretched out my arm and the fulmar turned its head, tilted its wings, and fell towards the waves.

'I thought I'd find you here,' said a familiar voice.

It was Elsie, holding on to her black beret with the palm of one hand, and scrunching the collar of her overcoat tightly together with the other. 'Dear me. It's a bit blowy,' she shouted.

'Just a bit.'

'Mind if I join you?'

'No. There's plenty of room. Everyone else is inside.'

'Yes, you're right. We're alone, quite alone.'

She clapped her hands together and walked over to the railings. 'Just look at those seagulls! I do love watching them dive.'

'They're gannets,' I said. 'If you look through your binoculars you'll see they're much bigger than seagulls and they've got yellow heads.'

'Gannets. Yes. How silly of me. I can see them quite clearly now.'

It had stopped raining. We were quiet for a bit. Just looking. Then she said, 'I do believe you can see the Orkneys.'

I looked out towards the front of the boat and where the pale grey sky met the dark grey sea, there were three or four grey humps of land.

'Oh, bother!'

I turned round. Elsie was leaning over the railing, trying to reach her black beret. It was dangling from the metal arm of a lifeboat holder that was leaning out over the side.

'This wind! Such a nuisance, I just can't *quite* reach it,' she said, getting all flustered.

'Let me try. If I stand on the railing I'll be able to get it.'

'No. That's far too dangerous.'

'Not if you hold on to my other arm when I lean out. Watch.'

And without waiting for an answer I climbed up onto the railing, grabbed her hand and leant out. For a split second I looked down and saw the side of the boat disappearing like a black cliff face into the clouds of foam. The wind was whistling in my ears.

I thought of the fulmar hanging in the air, how it had simply tilted its wings and disappeared. I stretched out my arm and grabbed the beret. I was turning to tell Elsie to pull me back in when I saw him. Francesco Allegretto was standing outside the door to the Observation Deck, staring at me. I saw his mouth moving, then Elsie gave a sharp tug and pulled me back onto the deck. When I looked back at the door he'd vanished.

'That was a close call,' said Elsie, dusting off her beret. 'I think perhaps we should step inside, before we have any more accidents.'

CHAPTER ELEVEN

Daydream Believer

The *St Ola* filled one half of Stromness harbour and brightly painted fishing boats, like the caravans of some visiting circus, bobbed colourfully in the other. It was half past five in the afternoon. The rain had stopped, the sky had cleared, and for the rest of the day the sun was going to shine.

'Now are you sure you're going to be all right?' asked Elsie. 'Will there be someone meeting you off the boat?'

'Not exactly.'

She gave me one of her downward-looking stares.

'I'm meeting someone on Hoy,' I said, looking

down at my feet. 'I'm going to try and get a boat across there this afternoon.'

'That might prove difficult.'

'Why's that?'

'The last ferry to Hoy left Stromness half an hour ago and there are no ferries running tomorrow. Tomorrow is Sunday and nothing runs in Scotland on a Sunday. Except the vicar, and that's only if he's late for church. So I'm afraid Monday morning will be the earliest you can get to Hoy.'

'I see,' I said thoughtfully.

'So you'll need to spend at least two nights in Stromness. I'm booked into the Stromness Hotel. I'm sure they'll be able to make room for one small boy. It might be a bit more expensive than the average guest house, but, in the circumstances, I'll be happy to help out.'

'No, honestly, there'll be plenty of B and Bs. I'll just take a walk and get myself fixed up.'

'Just as you like, Stanley. Anyway, we're bound to bump into each other again. I can feel it in my bones and my bones are never wrong.'

Elsie and I were among the last passengers to leave. I watched her climb the hill to the Stromness Hotel and spotted Francesco Allegretto heading in the same direction. I waited till they were both safely inside, then crossed the cobbled square in front of the harbour and turned left up the main street.

The shops and the houses were huddled together, their little windows peering out onto each other. Every so often there'd be a narrow gap and the silvery light of the sea would flicker between the dark walls. On the other side, the gaps led into narrow cobbled alleys that climbed steeply up the hillside.

It was all so different from anywhere else I'd ever been. I felt like an explorer, the same way I had when I first climbed the stairs to Neville's studio. At any moment I half expected to smell oil paint, but instead I smelled food and remembered that I hadn't eaten properly since breakfast. The sign said:

Paradise Café

(NO DIRTY BOOTS, NO WISECRACKS, NO DRUNKS!)

Proprietress: Eve Gunn

It was empty, there were no customers, but the door was wide open. I stepped cautiously inside, brushing against some tiny silver bells that were hanging from the doorframe. The quiet tinkling slowly died away. The walls were painted dark green and covered in paintings, mostly posters of exhibitions, but also some real ones in frames. There were about ten tables each with four chairs. The tables were covered with purple tablecloths and in the middle of each table there was a dark green candle and a little vase of white flowers. I walked to the end of the room and sat down at a table near the wall. Nobody came.

There was a little oil painting on the wall, just above where I was sitting. It looked familiar, like I'd seen it, or something like it, somewhere before. It was of a beach covered in round stones. The stones got bigger from right to left, the ones on the far left must have been the size of armchairs. Behind the beach, in the background, there were huge rounded hills that were purple and green like the café. There was a signature in the bottom right hand corner. I'd just stood up to read it when the bells by the door started tinkling.

A boy came in wheeling a bicycle and at the same time a woman appeared from behind some beaded curtains on the other side of the room.

'Round the back, mister. No bikes!'

'Aw, Mam.'

'Round the back! Don't, "Aw, Mam", me.'

She glared at him with bright green eyes, her red hair tied back in a ponytail. It was the lady I'd met briefly on the ferry. The boy slowly wheeled his bike out of the café, and only when he'd disappeared from view, did she turn round and see me.

'Well, hello there. So the wind didn't blow you away then?'

'No.'

'And you've found Paradise.'

'Pardon?'

'The café!'

'Oh, I see. Is it yours?'

'Aye. Proprietress, Eve Gunn, that's me. We're actually supposed to be closed, but "Mr Daydream Believer" probably left the door open.'

'I'm sorry,' I said, starting to get up.

'No. You stay right where you are,' she said, gently putting her hand on my shoulder. 'I'll just shut that door and then I'll fetch you a menu.'

'I don't want to be any trouble.'

'It's no trouble at all.'

It was kind of exciting being in a café by myself, being able to order whatever I wanted. No-one was leaning over my shoulder saying, 'That Black Forest Gateau's much too rich,' or, 'You can't possibly order Prawn Cocktails in the middle of the afternoon.' But, in the end, I chose a piece of apple pie and a glass of milk, figuring that was as close to 'no trouble' as you could get. Eve Gunn disappeared through the beaded curtains and five minutes later the boy came back, carrying a dark green plate and a glass of milk.

'My name's Ewart, what's yours?'

'Stanley.'

He stood there, staring at me, like he was trying to fit the name to the person.

'It means a stony field,' I said.

'Plenty of them round here.'

He put the apple pie and glass of milk down in front of me, pulled out a chair and sat down. He had red hair like his mum, but his eyes were grey and he wore glasses. His face was covered in freckles. I'd never seen that many before, not on one person. He was bigger than me and a bit tubby. I guessed he was my age, maybe a bit older.

'My mam says I'm to try and find out why you're by yourself, but I think it's none of her business. She's just being nosy. I mean, you might have all sorts of reasons for being by yourself, private reasons. Maybes you're an orphan, or an escaped convict, or maybes you've just run away from home to make your fortune.'

'I'm not running away.'

'But you're not from Orkney, and you're still by yourself.'

'So?'

'Exactly! It's none of her business. I'll tell her you're an orphan.'

'But I'm not.'

'Doesn't matter. I tell her all sorts of things to keep her quiet. An orphan's better than an escaped convict. You don't look like an escaped convict.'

'Do I look like an orphan?'

'A bit.'

'How come?'

'You look kind of lost, like you don't fit in, like you've got no friends.'

'I've got a friend on Hoy.'

'Hoy! I'm impressed. I thought I was the only person alive that knew anybody on Hoy. Nothing ever happens on Hoy, ever. There's not that much happens here, but compared to Hoy, Stromness is the centre of the universe.'

'What about those climbers a couple of weeks ago? The ones that climbed that rock tower for television?' I asked.

'The Old Man. I suppose so, but that's once in a blue moon. Have you seen that thing? It's straight up and down and falling to bits. They were nutters. I told them. They all came in here before they did it. They had my mam's lasagne for supper. I said, "You wouldn't catch me climbing that thing. Not for a million pounds. I'd rather be chased by loads of Apaches, all firing arrows and chucking tomahawks and things, trying to get my scalp".' And he grabbed a fistful of red hair. 'Did you see that John Wayne film last night?'

'No,' I said, 'I was on the train.'

'Pity. It was fantastic. John Wayne's a star. He can

strike a match with one hand and shoot Indians over his shoulder with the other, at the same time!'

I nodded and finished off the apple pie.

'I've been practising,' he said.

'Shooting Apaches?'

'No. Striking matches with one hand. I can nearly do it. But don't tell my mam. She'll kill me if she catches me playing with matches.'

I pushed the empty plate away and finished the milk.

'Whereabouts are you staying tonight?' he asked.

'I don't know. I've got to find somewhere.'

He picked up my plate and glass and disappeared through the beaded curtain. Two minutes later he was back.

'That's settled then,' he said.

'What's settled?'

'You're staying here, in "Paradise".'

'What did you tell your mum?'

'I told her you were an orphan. I said you used to live on a boat with your mother and father and eight baby sisters. And that you were all sailing round the world when one night a giant squid crept up on deck. And his huge long tentacles slithered inside the boat and dragged everyone, still sleeping, out of their beds and down to the bottom of the sea. All except you, because you were in the galley making a cup of tea. And when you came back it was just in time to see its slimy orange tentacles slipping silently over the side. You dropped your tea, grabbed an axe, and chopped one off that was the size of telegraph pole. But it was too late. They'd all gone. And you had to steer the boat all alone for days and days and weeks and weeks until you sighted land. But, at first, there wasn't any land. Just sea. Miles and miles of sea. And you ran out of food and all that was left to eat was the slimy orange tentacle of the giant squid. So each day you sliced a bit off and ate it raw to stay alive and you swore that, if ever you found dry land again, you'd never ever leave it and you'd never ever eat squid again. And then one day, after you'd eaten the very last bit of tentacle, you saw the Isle of Hoy in the distance and you decided that that's where you were going to live. But first you came to Stromness for some apple pie to get rid of the taste of squid.'

'What did she say?'

'She said it was the biggest load of rubbish she'd ever heard and that squid was quite tasty and you could have the spare bed in my room.'

That night, when we were lying in our beds, I told Ewart the whole story. I'd been dying to tell somebody. I'd kept the lid on everything for what seemed like ages and once I took it off it all rushed out: about Neville, and the flood, and the gallery in London, and hearing the dealers plotting to have him killed.

Then about meeting Francesco Allegretto on the train. Even about Elsie Robinson.

He lay on his side, listening without saying a word, and when I'd finished he turned over and fell asleep.

CHAPTER TWELVE

Yellow Submarine

'I've been thinking,' said Ewart.

'About what?' I asked.

'About that story you told me last night. That friend of yours, Neville Whatshisname.'

'And?'

'Well, I was just thinking Hoy's not such a big island, but it's big enough. You could waste a lot of time looking for someone, especially if that someone didn't want to be found. And then I started thinking, if he's been painting all these paintings of the Old Man, the chances are he's staying somewhere nearby and that has to be Rackwick.'

'Why?'

"'Cause there's nowhere else for miles. There's hardly anybody there as it is. There's just this beach with great massive round stones on and these massive cliffs, but it's only a few miles from the Old Man. The thing is, I've got an uncle lives there, Uncle Gordon. At least, he's my mam's uncle really, which makes him my great uncle, but ordinary "uncle" seems to do.'

'Maybe I should go there first and ask him if he's seen Neville.'

'No good,' said Ewart, shaking his head.

'How come?'

'Uncle Gordon's kind of strange. If he doesn't know you, he won't speak to you. He's a bit of a hermit, a castaway. He doesn't have a telephone, or a telly, or anything like that. He spends all day walking along the cliff tops or beachcombing. He reckons that he can survive on seagulls' eggs and what he finds washed up. He found a sack of coffee beans once. And another time he found ten pairs of brand new shoes, except they were all size thirteen, and he's only an eight. He keeps a list of all the things he finds in this book. It's like a diary. He reckons that, over the years, he's picked up nearly a hundred orange rubber gloves. Mostly left hands. No, it's no use expecting to get much sense out of Uncle Gordon. I'll have to come along with you. He'll talk to me.'

It was Sunday morning. I wanted to be moving, I wanted to be doing something, but Stromness was dead, even the seagulls were quiet. We were sitting with our legs dangling over the edge of the harbour wall. Ewart had a box of matches. He was practising his John Wayne trick. He'd hold the box in his left hand; push it open with his left thumb; swivel it round so that it fitted snugly in his palm; reach in with his left thumb and forefinger and pull out a match – all just using one hand. Then he'd close the box with his left little finger; turn it over so that the sandpaper edge was up, and still holding the match between his left forefinger and thumb, drag it along the sandpaper till it burst into flames. Then he'd look over his shoulder and shoot an imaginary Apache with two fingers.

The box was almost empty, he was getting quite good, he'd only burnt himself twice. He was dropping the lighted matches into the sea below. There was a whole fleet of them floating on the surface. Behind us some seagulls started squawking. I looked over my shoulder. No Apaches, just the dark shadow of the Stromness Hotel. And a cold shiver ran through me as I imagined Francesco Allegretto pulling aside a curtain with his metal claw, and watching us from one of the windows.

'I'm not making any of this up,' I said. 'If you do come to Hoy, it could be really dangerous.'

'Great. The more dangerous the better. We can be secret agents. And Neville can be the mad professor with the plans for the rocket. And that Italian feller, Francesco Alligator, can be a spy trying to steal them. And unless we can stop him, he's going to blow up the world.'

'Ewart, he's here to *kill* Neville.'

'Even better. There's no time to waste. If he gets to Neville first it'll really spoil things.'

'No kidding.'

'We've got to keep one step ahead. The first ferry to Hoy's tomorrow morning, but I reckon we can cadge a lift across there tonight.'

'That would be great. How?'

'Well, there's a full moon tonight, so we *ought* to go in by submarine. Then get shot out of the torpedo tubes wearing black scuba gear. And have blackened faces, and knives strapped to our legs. And spear guns. But we'll make do with the *Storm Finch*.'

'What's that?'

'It's John MacNeal's old lobster boat. He goes out to Hoy every night about six to check his pots.'

'D'you think he'll give us a lift?'

'No problem. John does very nicely selling his lobsters to the Stromness Hotel. If the word gets round that the Stromness Hotel's full of spies killing people, it'll be bad for business. It's my mam that's the problem. She never believes a word I say. Maybes I'll just tell her we're going to visit Uncle Gordon and leave it at that.'

*　　*　　*

It was a good haul. There were twelve big lobsters clattering around the bottom of the boat, like knights in armour that had fallen off their horses. I'd expected them to be orange like the one in Neville's Ford Cortina, but that's only when they're cooked. When they come out of the sea they're a dark purply-blue with creamy white freckles and bright red whiskers a mile long. I felt real sorry for them, but business is business.

Rackwick Bay was on the other side of Hoy. There was a single track road, but no buses and hardly any cars. It was quicker for us to follow a narrow path that snaked between the hills. The hills were massive, the same shape that animals make when they curl up to go to sleep. You could almost hear them breathing.

It was eight o'clock by the time we reached Rackwick. The path we were on joined up with the road. We followed it down to the sea and climbed to the top of some sand dunes. There were two massive cliffs at either end of the bay and huge waves were rolling in and smashing against them, sending great clouds of white spray *whooshing* into the air.

The breeze was fresher now. The sea shone silver, but out near the horizon there was a band of dark blue where you could see the rain falling.

'Looks like we might get some weather,' said Ewart.

'Where's your Uncle Gordon's house?'

'That's it up there,' he said, pointing to a small white-washed croft with a green turf roof, perched on the edge of the northern-most cliff. 'He calls it "The Eyrie". You can see why. There can't be many eagles with a better view than Uncle Gordon. If he's home, chances are, he's already seen us. He'll be spying on us through his binoculars.'

We clambered down the dunes and began walking along the beach towards The Eyrie. The beach was covered in stones. They were smooth and round like eggs. The further we walked the bigger they grew until some of them were the size of armchairs. The breeze had turned into a proper wind and the light was beginning to fade. Back inland, the hills had darkened and seemed to have shrunk back, like they were getting ready for the storm. It all felt strangely familiar.

'Some sea to make these, eh?' said Ewart, nodding down at one of the armchair-sized boulders. 'Uncle Gordon says that, when the real storms come in winter, you can hear these big'uns being rolled round and round. He says it can keep you awake all night. It sounds like scrunching glass marbles in your fist, with your fist right next to your ear. But he says that after ten years, or so, you get used to it.'

CHAPTER THIRTEEN

Midnight Confessions

There was a family of white ducks sitting on the grass roof, huddled round the chimney, keeping warm. Ewart knocked on the door. No answer. He knocked again. Still no answer.

'Maybes he's out collecting. Let's take a look round the back.'

Round the back was a vegetable garden surrounded by a fence made from bits of driftwood. Almost every bit had an orange rubber glove stuck on the end. In the wind, it was like loads of orange hands waving madly.

'See what I mean?' said Ewart.

We waited there, trying to stay out of the wind,

which was now blowing from the sea in angry gusts. After several failed attempts to count the orange gloves, a lonely figure appeared, trudging up the path from the beach. He wore a red woollen hat, an old brown duffel coat, and two wellies, not exactly a pair, because one was black and the other was green. It was Uncle Gordon. He was pulling a trolley behind him made from planks of wood and old pram wheels. It was stacked high with interesting bits of driftwood and various empty plastic bottles. He stopped at the gate and stared at us.

'Hello, Uncle Gordon,' said Ewart.

Uncle Gordon nodded. He put his hand deep inside his duffel-coat pocket and pulled out an orange rubber glove.

'Ninety-nine,' he said, placing it with the others on the end of the fence.

'This is my friend Stanley. We're looking for this feller called Neville Windsomething. We think he's here in Rackwick. He paints pictures of the Old Man, but he's just pretending. Really he's this mad professor that's invented these X-ray specs. And, when you wear them you can make things explode just by looking. And there's this Italian feller, Francesco Alligator, or something. He's trying to steal the specs and sell them to the Russians. And we've got to stop him before it's too late.'

If Uncle Gordon had heard of Neville, he wasn't letting on. He was watching the fingers of the orange gloves flutter in the wind. I guessed that he was used to Ewart's lively imaginings.

'You'll be hungry,' said Uncle Gordon.

'Starving,' said Ewart.

'Fish pie?'

'Great.'

'Tatties and carrots?'

'Great.'

'Best get digging then. Storm's coming. Ten minutes. Fifteen at the most.'

He pulled a long handled fork out of the ground and handed it to Ewart. Then he opened the door and went inside.

'Don't mind him,' said Ewart. 'He's always like that with people he doesn't know, pretends they're not there. He's not likely to tell us anything about Neville until after supper. He's a great cook though. That was his job. He was a cook on a deep sea trawler for twenty years. He's famous for inventing a way for doing eggs in a stormy sea.'

'How?'

'You get some slices of bread and make holes in the middle. Then you fry them till they're stuck to the bottom of the pan, crack in your eggs so that they drop into the holes and spread over the bread and then there's no way they can slide out of the pan, even when the waves are twenty foot high. "Eggs à la Gordon" they're called.'

Ewart pushed the fork deep down near one of the potato plants. He leant back on the long handle and eased up a large clump of black sandy soil. Nestling inside were a dozen white potatoes, smooth and round, like the stones on the beach.

'There's a bucket over there,' said Ewart.

I fetched the bucket and dropped them in. We pulled up some carrots, then went inside.

The Eyrie was basically two rooms with a tiny kitchen, known as the galley, sandwiched in between. Ewart seemed to know his way around. So I followed him through into one of the end rooms.

The walls were made from huge stones, piled one on top of the other. Inside they'd been painted with white gloss paint, so that they sparkled in the fire-light. The ceiling was varnished wood and shaped like an up-turned boat. At one end of the room there was a wood-burning stove and at the other, an old box bed that seemed to be holding up the roof. There were shelves made out of grey driftwood crammed with books and records.

Uncle Gordon appeared in the doorway. He'd taken off his red woolly hat and his white hair looked like it was glad to be free. He was holding what, at first, I thought was a shiny black dinner plate, but turned out to be an old gramophone record. He wiped it on the sleeve of his jumper and wound up an ancient record player.

'Did you find that today on the beach?' asked Ewart.

'No. I borrowed it last week . . . from a friend.'

Uncle Gordon put the gramophone record on the player and slowly lowered the arm. There was a crackling like hot fat, then Jelly Roll Morton started up. Uncle Gordon looked at me with black beady eyes beneath bushy white eyebrows, and smiled.

He told us that Neville had arrived at Rackwick Bay just over a year ago. He'd bought a croft for two thousand pounds further up the hillside. All his provisions were brought across on the ferry and delivered once a week. He kept himself to himself and hardly spoke to anyone, except Uncle Gordon. The pair of them had lots in common: cooking, jazz, and a suspicious nature.

Neville told Gordon he'd come to Hoy to find something, something that was missing in his life, something he'd once had, but then lost. He hadn't even heard about the floods back home until months afterwards and by then he was definitely missing, presumed dead, and suddenly famous. They'd had a good laugh about it. Even Uncle Gordon had seen the funny side. It was Patrick Fitzwilliam that had seen the other possibilities: higher prices, huge profits etc.

He'd persuaded Neville to lie low and keep painting. But the truth was, Neville didn't need much persuading. He was having too good a time. He wasn't going to 'come back from the dead' until he was good and ready.

When I told Uncle Gordon at supper time, about the gallery directors plotting to have Neville killed, it sounded only slightly more believable than Ewart's X-ray specs. But I could tell by the way he stared at his plate that he was listening. I knew we were probably one step ahead of Francesco Allegretto, but I still wanted to see Neville as quickly as possible. It seemed crazy to have come all this way just to sit down and eat fish pie, when I was so close.

'You've an honest face, Stanley, which is more than I can say for Ewart Gunn, here.'

Ewart smiled and winked.

'We'll sort Neville out in the morning. There'll be no-one on the hill on a night like this, and that includes your fancy-pants hired killers. Now tell me young Ewart, does your mother know where you are?'

'Yes.'

'And is she still ... "alone at the helm", so to speak.'

'Yes.'

'Ach. That's a terrible waste. And her, the best-looking woman in Orkney.'

The table fell quiet, but outside the rain beat on the

glass of the window, like somebody trying to get in.

All night long the storm raged around The Eyrie. The wind roared in from out at sea, battering at the door, and howling down the chimney of the wood-burning stove. It was hard to get to sleep. Apart from the noises, there were a million things on my mind. Ewart and I sat up till late in the old box bed, riding out the storm below deck.

'Uncle Gordon says that, in the old days, the folks that lived at Rackwick were "wreckers". It's there in the name, "Rack"'s a wreck, "Wick"'s a bay. "Bay of the Wreck", get it?'

'Yes, but how were they "wreckers"?' I asked.

'When there was a storm at night, like this one, they'd go down to the shore and light lamps. Any boats that were in trouble would see the lights shining and aim between them, expecting to beach the boats on the sand.'

'That's not "wrecking" though.'

'It is when you hang the lamps on either side of the big cliff. By the time the poor sods saw where they were, it was too late. The waves would just toss them in and they'd smash to pieces on the rocks. And the "wreckers" would be there to grab anything that was washed up.'

'What happened to the sailors?'

'Drowned probably.'

'That's terrible!'

'I know, but it's like Uncle Gordon says, it's the times that were terrible. And terrible times make terrible folk. If it wasn't for the odd wreck, the folks at Rackwick might have starved. Creative beach-combing, he calls it.'

'Has he ever . . . ?'

'Not as far as I know.'

The wind whistled eerily down the chimney.

'Ewart?'

'Yes?'

'Where's your dad?'

Ewart pushed his glasses back up to the top of his nose, and shrugged his shoulders.

'*My* dad died four years ago,' I said. 'His appendix burst. I live with my mum and little sister.'

Ewart was quiet. He lay on his front, staring into the flames of the wood-burning stove, thinking about what I'd just told him. Then he sat up, took off his glasses, and blinked at the fire.

'I don't know whether my dad's dead or not. My mam used to tell me he was lost at sea. She used to tell me he was a famous explorer and that, one day, he'd come back with all sorts of treasure. When he didn't she started saying that he must have drowned, or been eaten by sharks. But that was when I was little. When I was bigger she told me the truth, which was that he'd run away because he was too scared to get married. I suppose that makes me a bastard.'

'I'm sorry.'

'Don't be. I'm not bothered. No-one says anything at school. It was worse when I had to start wearing glasses. They all called me "Specky Four-eyes". I hated it. I didn't want to go back to school. I told me mam and she said, "You go back tomorrow. And the first boy that opens his mouth, hit him!" So I did.'

'What happened?'

'He hit me back and broke my glasses.'

'What did your mum say?'

'Nothing. She took me to the optician's and bought me a new pair, then sent me back to school.'

'And?'

'No more "Specky Four-eyes". It's my mam I feel sorry for . . . It's the big joke in Stromness, that Eve's in Paradise without Adam. That's why she's got "NO WISE-CRACKS" on the sign. It's daft. I mean, I know she's got a temper, but she's a good cook. There must be plenty of fellers would put up with the shouting for free apple pie and strawberry ice cream.'

We lay very still, and through the wind and the rain, I was sure I could hear the sound of glass marbles scrunching together.

CHAPTER FOURTEEN

First There is a Mountain

When I woke up the sun was shining. Uncle Gordon was in the garden inspecting the storm damage. There were two broken plant pots and a dead seagull in the cabbages. The seagull had a broken neck, but the cabbages were fine. The rubber gloves drooped on their fence posts, exhausted after a night of flapping about. They all seemed to be still there.

'A bit blowy last night,' said Uncle Gordon, throwing the dead seagull over the fence. 'Sleep well?'

'Too well,' I said, looking down at my watch and slapping at my face where a midgie was biting.

'I was going to wake you both earlier, but the

midgies were terrible. There's a few about now, right enough. But earlier . . . ach! I've never known them so bad. And I've seen them drive cattle over the cliff edge. There was no wind, you see. None at all. It blew itself out last night. And that's just how the midgies like it. First thing in the morning, and last thing at night. Wee piranhas with wings. They'd have eaten you alive, if you'd so much as poked your head out the door.'

'Which house does Neville live in?'

'That wee croft up there. It's called The Crow's Nest, what with it being the highest in Rackwick.'

I peered up the hillside to where the sunlight was twinkling on some glass.

'He had those windows put in the roof when he first bought the place. I thought he must be one of those stargazers, but it's for his painting. He needs the light.'

'Can we go up there now?'

'No point. He'll be over at the Old Man by now. He's been painting that daft bit of rock almost every day since he arrived.'

'How do I get there?'

'Give young Ewart a shout and I'll take you there myself.'

We scrambled up the steep hillside until we met a black peaty path that wound its way northwards along the coast. To the east, the hills were dark and the sky was light. To the west, the sea was light and the sky was dark. It was like being in two different places at once, walking a tightrope between them. And all the time I was thinking, Neville's just been along here. These are his footprints!

After about an hour I saw the Old Man for the first time, poking up from beyond the edge of a distant cliff. It was exactly like Ewart had said, 'straight up and down and falling to bits'.

'What d'you think?' asked Ewart.

'It's amazing. It doesn't look possible.'

'Five hundred feet from top t' bottom, or so they tell me,' said Uncle Gordon.

'How's it stay up?'

'It used to be a massive arch,' said Ewart, 'with a bridge of rock that went from the top all the way over to the edge of the cliff. You could have walked across it. But it fell down ages ago. I wish I'd been there when it went. *Imagine!* There's lumps of rock down there the size of double-decker buses. I dare you to look over the edge.'

'Careful!' warned Uncle Gordon, 'If you're going anywhere near that edge, get down on your hands and knees and crawl *reeaal* slowly. The wee puffins make their nests in the old rabbit burrows and they do a grand job of digging them out. The edge of this cliff is fair riddled with tunnels that are forever collapsing. If you're standing on top of one when it goes, you'll be over before you've time to curse the puffin that dug it.'

Ewart and I crawled slowly forwards and lay on our bellies with our heads over the edge. A cool blast of salty air rushed up and hit our faces. I squinted down through spiralling dots of seagulls. The air was thick with them, like a swarm of white bees. The sea was deep green with a giant spider's web of white foam spreading out from the foot of the Old Man. Slowly I began to look up. Up from the sea, up through the gulls, up the dark red tower, higher and higher until I had to roll over on my back as the top narrowed into a black spearhead of rock. I shut my eyes. I'd just looped the loop. I was sweating and shivery cold, all at the same time.

'Are you all right, Stanley?' asked Uncle Gordon.

I wasn't sure so I didn't answer.

'You've gone as white as a gull,' said Ewart, 'No head for heights, eh?'

'Back here you two,' said Uncle Gordon. 'You'll not see Neville from there anyway. He's round here.'

We followed him further round the headland to where the cliffs weren't quite so steep and there was a bit of a path going down to a grassy ledge. From the ledge you could see the whole of the Old Man, from top to bottom. And there, sitting with his back to us on an old wooden fishing box, wearing his baggy brown jumper, was Neville.

I stood at the top of the path, unable to move. After all that time of telling myself that he was still alive, after coming all this way, it was still like seeing a ghost. But then 'the ghost' moved. He lifted up a large canvas he'd been working on and lay it, face up, beside him on the heather. Then he began to clean his brushes, wiping them on the grass.

'Neville!' I shouted.

'It's no use,' said Uncle Gordon, pointing to the sky. 'The wind. He'll not hear you up here. You'll need to go down there. Mind the path, it's a wee bit steep. Ewart'll go with you, I'd best be getting back. There's a whole beach waiting to be combed after last night's storm and who knows what we'll find washed up? Tell Neville, if he needs me, he knows where to find me.'

Uncle Gordon left and Ewart and I started down the path. Ewart was in front, I was behind. It was steeper and trickier than it looked, because last night's rain had softened the mud. Eventually, we got to the grassy ledge. The wind was swirling round the Old Man and the gulls were swirling with it.

Neville still had his back to us. I was close enough to smell the fresh oil paint when I suddenly had an awful thought . . . What if he didn't want to see me? What if he just wanted to be left alone? But then I remembered Francesco Allegretto. Ewart, who'd been in front, stepped round behind me and nudged me forward. I heard myself say, 'Neville.'

He didn't turn round straightaway. He froze, as if me saying his name had turned him into stone. Then, very slowly, he turned round. His pale grey eyes blinking in disbelief through the big, round 'owl' glasses. And his face was split from ear to ear with the biggest, broadest grin imaginable.

'*STANLEY!*' he shouted and threw the paintbrush he was holding over his shoulder. It spiralled through the air, getting smaller and smaller, falling out of sight into the chasm of screaming gulls. 'Is it really you?' he asked, grabbing me by the shoulders. Then he looked over at Ewart.

'This is my friend Ewart. His Great-Uncle Gordon's your neighbour.'

Neville nodded. Ewart didn't say anything.

'This is fantastic! I can't believe it. What, I mean, how . . . ?'

But Neville's voice was drowned by more screaming from the gulls. He glanced up at the Old Man and then down at the canvas lying on top of the heather.

'Let me pack this lot away. We'll go back to The Crow's Nest. It's a bit quieter.'

Neville threw his paints and brushes and other bits and pieces into a rucksack. Then he tied the canvas to the back so that the wet oil paint was facing outwards. When I looked around I saw he'd left his mark. The flat rock he'd used for mixing his colours on was a mass of paint splodges. There was paint on the grass, paint on the fishing box and paint in his hair. It was the same old Neville.

We retraced our steps back along the path towards Rackwick Bay. I walked in front with Neville, Ewart trailed behind. He was strangely quiet. He hadn't said a word since we'd first clapped eyes on Neville. You'd have thought *he'd* seen the ghost and not me.

'They all think you're dead,' I began.

'I know. At least, I didn't know until I saw the newspapers, and then I couldn't understand why you hadn't told them.'

'*Me?* How could I?'

'That note I left, pinned to the beehive. I explained about needing to get away. How I thought I'd come up here to—'

'*Look in the mirror.*'

'That's right.'

'The rain had washed it away, all except the last words. It didn't make sense.'

'Oh. I see. So you also thought . . .'

'Yes. I did for a bit. Not at first. But when I got the invitation from the gallery to that exhibition in London and it said the "late" Neville Windrush, I did then.'

'I'm sorry. I'm *really* sorry. I didn't realize. I just assumed . . . The exhibition was Patrick's idea. He and Donald were the only people who knew where I was. It all seemed like a bit of a laugh. But you know all this. I sent you that letter. I gave it to Patrick when he came to visit me. He said he'd post it to you when he got back.'

'I never got a letter.'

'Then how . . . ?'

That's when I told Neville. I told him everything. I told him about overhearing Patrick Fitzwilliam and Donald Abercromby downstairs in the gallery plotting to have him killed. I told him about the train journey and how I'd met Francesco Allegretto. And I told him how Ewart had helped me get to Hoy and how we'd spent last night with Uncle Gordon at The Eyrie. He listened in silence, every now and then stopping and shaking his head in disbelief. By the time I'd finished talking we'd veered off up the hillside and The Crow's Nest was in sight.

'How d'you like it?' asked Neville. 'I thought I'd call it The Crow's Nest to remind me of the Old Mill. Remember the crows? I've always had a soft spot for crows.'

I suppose I'd been expecting him to panic, or at least be a bit concerned, but instead he was talking about crows! Either he didn't believe me, or he didn't *want* to believe me.

CHAPTER FIFTEEN

The Fool on the Hill

'MMMMMMEEEEEEEOOOOOOWWWWWWWW
WWWWWWW!'

'He thinks you've brought his liver,' said Neville.

It was Vincent. In all the excitement of seeing Neville again, I'd completely forgotten to ask about Vincent. He limped across and head-butted my leg.

'What's wrong with his paw?' I asked, bending down and combing my fingers through his fur.

'Thorn, I think,' said Neville. 'I've bathed it and had a look, but I can't see anything.'

'Some cat,' said Ewart. 'What's he eat, sheep?'

'No, rabbits mostly. He catches them himself. They have burrows on the cliff tops, right on the edge. It doesn't bear thinking about, him at his age, chasing rabbits along the clifftops. I don't know about nine lives, I reckon when they were handing lives out, they threw in an extra ninety for old Vincent here.'

Neville opened the door and we stepped inside. The Crow's Nest had been knocked through into one long room, which Neville had as a studio, with a kitchen at one end and a bed at the other. There were paintings everywhere, mostly views of the Old Man. They were good. I liked them straight away.

'*Phworr!* What's that stink?' whispered Ewart.

'Oil paint,' I whispered back.

'Take a seat, boys,' said Neville, pointing to an ancient-looking sofa, that was leaning against the far wall. 'Watch where you're putting your feet.'

We sat down. It was like coming home; the puddles of paint, the crumpled tubes, the buckets full of brushes, the empty bottles and fags ends. Neville took off his rucksack, untied the new painting, and propped it up on an empty easel that was standing in the middle of the room.

'There! Not bad, eh? Ten thousand quid for a morning's work. Let's have three teas. Hang the expense!'

'Is he serious?' asked Ewart.

'About the teas?'

'No. The painting.'

'Yes. He's serious.'

'You mean somebody's going to pay *ten thousand quid* to hang that on their wall?'

'Probably,' I said, suddenly feeling defensive. 'He's *really* famous. They'll be queuing up round the block for these back in London.'

'Nutters!'

'What's the matter? Don't you like them?'

'They're all right. But ten thousand quid? You could probably buy half of Hoy for that.'

I checked my watch. It was nearly two o'clock. Plenty of time for anyone to have caught the first ferry from Stromness and be in Rackwick.

'He doesn't believe you, does he?' whispered Ewart.

'What about?'

'About Francesco Alligator coming to get him.'

'I don't think so.'

'It was just a game, wasn't it?'

'No!'

'Come on. It's getting boring. No-one's getting killed or anything. If we're going to pretend, we can pretend better than this. Look at all these paintings, they've got to be worth a fortune. We could be international art thieves. And this could be a famous museum. And . . .'

'Sugar?' asked Neville.

'No, thanks.'

'Four, please,' shouted Ewart.

Neville came back with the teas. He sat down on a stool in front of his new painting. No-one spoke. Vincent curled up by my feet, licking his paw. Everyone was thinking their own thoughts. Ewart was probably working out how to get the paintings through the skylight to the helicopter that was hovering overhead. I was wondering how I could convince Neville that I was telling the truth. And Neville was rolling a fag. When he'd finished he took a box of matches from his jeans pocket and did the John Wayne trick of opening it and striking a match with one hand.

'I can do that,' said Ewart.

'Do what?'

'Light a match with one hand. Just like John Wayne when he's being chased by Apaches. He's got the horse's reins in one hand and the matches in the other. He lights his fag, puts the reins between his teeth, and shoots the—'

But Ewart didn't get any further, because the flame had reached Neville's fingertips.

'*Yeowww!*' he yelled, dropping the matches and lunging down to try and catch them.

It must have been exactly then, when Neville lunged downwards, that the bullet crashed through a window in the opposite wall and embedded itself, with a dull thud, in the wall above our heads. Bits of plaster trickled down and settled like dandruff on our shoulders. There was a flash of ginger fur, as Vincent made a quick exit.

'What was that?' asked Neville, staring wide-eyed at the broken window.

'Someone's chucking stones,' said Ewart, sounding a bit worried.

I looked up at the small crater in the plaster wall.

'Look at this!' said Neville.

He was pointing at a neat round hole, about the size of a jacket button, that had suddenly appeared in the top right-hand corner of his new painting. He sat on his stool, looked over his shoulder at the broken window, and then back at the hole. He put the tip of his finger in the hole and began to draw an imaginary line between the hole and the broken window. His finger moved slowly towards his head, until it was pointing right between his eyes.

'Hell's teeth!' he cried. And dived to the floor.

It was chaos. Everybody was scrabbling about, but nobody knew where to go.

'What's happening?' shouted Ewart, 'What's happening?'

'They're trying to kill me,' gasped Neville. 'They're really trying to kill me!'

'It's not for real, is it?' pleaded Ewart.

'That hole's real. That broken window's real. How much more "real" do you want?' asked Neville in a state of panic.

'I don't want to be here,' Ewart whimpered.

'Me neither,' agreed Neville, putting an arm round his shoulder.

I was as scared as anybody else. We were all looking towards the door, waiting for Francesco Allegretto to burst in. But nothing happened. Everything was quiet. There was just the soft hiss of the blue gas flames and the faint whistling of the kettle that Neville had forgotten to turn off.

CHAPTER SIXTEEN

Both Sides Now

When nothing happened we all started to feel a bit braver. We stood up and moved slowly towards the door, being careful not to stand in front of any windows. Neville turned off the gas.

'I think he's gone, don't you?' he said hopefully.

'I think so,' I agreed, 'I think he'd have been here by now if he was coming in.'

'I can't believe it. I just *can't* believe it,' sighed Neville.

'Maybes it was an accident,' suggested Ewart, blinking nervously.

'No,' I said emphatically.

'Stanley's right,' said Neville, 'there was nothing

accidental about that shot. A split-second earlier and I'd have . . . He must have come across from Stromness on the first ferry, found The Crow's Nest empty and hidden in the bracken outside until we came back. The thing I don't understand, is why he didn't just step out and shoot me. Why did he wait until I was inside?'

'He probably wasn't expecting us two,' I said, nodding towards Ewart. 'He'd have recognized me from the train. We'd have been witnesses, unless . . .'

'Unless what?' asked Ewart.

'Unless he killed all three of us.'

The Crow's Nest fell silent.

'Where d'you think he is now?' asked Ewart.

'I think he'll be heading back down the road to catch the ferry. He'll not want to hang about on Hoy. As far as he knows the bullet went straight through Neville's head. That's what it must have looked like from outside. Neville's dead, the job's done. He'll be off back to Italy for a decent cup of coffee,' I said.

'If that's all he wanted, I could have made him one here,' mumbled Neville.

'Does that mean he's going to get away?' asked Ewart.

'We should tell the police,' said Neville. 'Come to think of it, why didn't you tell the police before?'

'They'd never have believed me.'

'You're right. Even I didn't believe you. But now

we've got evidence – the bullet's got to be some-where in that wall. There's a phone box at the end of the road, down by the beach. If we call Stromness police they could pick him up off the ferry and hold him until they've had time to come out here and look for themselves.

We stepped outside. The place was deserted. Everything looked so still it could have been a photo-graph. Then a little breeze ruffled the bracken and a skylark flew up singing its head off. I felt my eyes creeping round the back of my head. I wasn't totally convinced that Francesco Allegretto had gone. There was just a chance he might still be lurking some-where, waiting to jump out. We tiptoed across the grass and into the waist-high bracken. Every swish was like an alarm bell going off.

We all started running. The others were slower. I left them behind and didn't stop until I reached the phone box. I pulled open the door, picked up the tele-phone, and began dialling, 9 . . . 9 . . .

It was dead.

I looked down at my feet and saw that the cable had been cut with a sharp knife. It hung down from the receiver, as lifeless as the green apple skin 'snake' that lay coiled on the floor.

'What'd . . . the . . . police . . . say?' panted Neville.

'Nothing. Phone's dead, he's cut the line.'

'How d'you know it was him?'

'There's his calling card,' I said, pointing down at the green apple 'snake'.

'So much for "Keep Britain Tidy",' joked Neville, but he was looking glum.

'What time's the next ferry to Stromness?' I asked.

'Half past three,' said Neville.

'And after that?'

'Half past five. That's the last one.'

'That's two and a half hours away. We could make it easy.'

'What's the rush?' asked Ewart. 'What happens if we bump into "you know who"?'

'He'll have left the island by the time we get there. He'll be catching the half past three boat. He'll have a car or something. Hit-men don't walk,' I said.

'But you don't *know*, do you?' said Ewart.

'Ewart's right,' said Neville, 'we're all just guessing. Our "friend" could be anywhere. For all we know, he's had second thoughts about that shot through the window and he's on his way back right now to double-check.'

We all turned and looked back down the road.

'Shouldn't we be hiding somewhere until we're sure he's gone?' said Ewart. 'Maybes over with Uncle Gordon.'

'That's not a bad idea,' said Neville, 'but . . .'

'But, what?'

'I'd rather not involve anyone else. It's me he's

after, not you. The safest place for you is as far away from me as possible, and that means getting you off this island.'

'That means catching the ferry,' said Ewart.

'I know, but if you go back over the top of Ward Hill, instead of using the road or the path, you'll be safe. When you get to the other end you'll be looking down on to Moaness pier. If the coast is clear you can catch the last ferry.'

'What'll you do?'

'I'll make myself scarce for a while. There's an empty croft above the cliffs at the other end of the bay. You can't see if from the road, or the beach. There isn't even a proper path, just an old sheep track that's waist-deep in heather. I'll stay there until I hear that Francesco Alligator's either in Stromness Police Station or back in sunny Italy.'

'How'll you know?'

'You'll have to tell me. You'll have to come back and find me. Just like you'll have to if anything goes wrong. It's not that hard to find when you know where it is and I'll leave you a note if, for any reason, I'm not there.'

'Don't leave it outside in the rain.'

'No,' he said, taking off his glasses and blinking nervously while he wiped them clean with the bottom of his jumper. 'Now you two had better get your skates on. Ward Hill's no doddle. It'll take you the best part of two hours to get from end to end.'

There didn't seem to be any alternative. Ewart and I went one way and Neville went the other. After twenty minutes or so I stopped and looked back and thought that I saw the lonely figure of Neville on the beach, jumping from boulder to boulder.

CHAPTER SEVENTEEN

A Whiter Shade of Pale

Ewart and I didn't talk much, we just kept going.
It was hard work. The heather at the bottom was
the worst, it was waist-deep and scratched your legs.
I was wearing jeans so it wasn't that bad, but Ewart
was wearing shorts and it took him ages. The higher
we climbed the steeper it became so that we had to
pull ourselves up on the long stringy branches and
when the heather thinned out there was just black
squidgey peat and bright green moss that you had to
dig your hands and feet into. Brown water oozed out
and trickled down our arms. Some of the moss was
red, like it had been soaking up blood.

When we reached the top it flattened out. There

was nothing for miles, nothing but broken bits of pale grey stone and scattered white bones. Up in the sky there was the black silhouette of an eagle, circling and watching. It was the kind of place that people in films died in.

'I'm starving and dying of thirst,' said Ewart.

'Me too.'

'D'y'think we'll make it across this desert? Or d'y'think they'll just find our skeletons picked clean by the vultures?' he asked, kicking at the skull of what might have been a rabbit or a hare.

'I think we'll survive.'

'I know, but just say we didn't. Just say we died of thirst and it took them ages to find our bodies. And by then all our flesh had been eaten by wild animals and our clothes had blown away. How would they know it was us?'

'Dental records.'

'You mean teeth?'

'Yes. Everyone's teeth are different and dentists can tell whose are whose.'

'Like the police with fingerprints?'

'Suppose so, except fingerprints disappear but teeth last for ever.'

'Nothing lasts for ever.'

'No.'

'I hate the dentist's. I can't imagine anything worse than being a dentist. There's this fellow in Stromness called "Dave The Grave". He's an undertaker. That's pretty weird. He drives round all day in this big black car with coffins in the back. He's seen loads of dead people. He reckons that after you're dead your hair keeps growing. If you've got any left.'

'Have you ever thought about dying?' I asked.

'Millions of times.'

'Do you ever wonder what it'll be like?'

'Depends how you go. Getting slowly crushed in a car-press or eaten alive by rats has got to be different from falling asleep in bed when you're ninety-nine.'

'I mean after.'

'Like heaven?'

'Maybe.'

'No. Not much. What about you?'

'Ages ago, when I was little, just after my dad died, I was lying in bed. It was the middle of the night and it was black dark. The kind of dark where it doesn't make any difference whether your eyes are open or closed. I knew my dad was dead because everyone said so and my mum hadn't stopped crying for weeks, but I still couldn't believe he wasn't there. I couldn't believe that he'd just *stopped* and everything else was going on like normal. I wanted to be with him more than anything, so I shut my eyes and thought myself dead. I imagined everything coming to a stop, until there was nothing left to think about.

Nothing in front and nothing behind. There was just this great gaping blackness and I was standing there, on the edge of it, looking down. I got really scared and opened my eyes, but it was still the same blackness. I thought I was dead. I thought I'd done it.'

The eagle followed us the length of Ward Hill and we arrived at the other end at twenty-five to six, just in time to see the last ferry leave Moaness pier. Three miles away, across the sea, the rooftops of Stromness were glinting in the sun.

'Aw, no!' moaned Ewart. 'What're we going to do now?'

'I don't know,' I said, feeling like my feet were set in concrete, 'start walking back, I suppose.'

'I want t'be home. I want my mum's lasagne and apple pie and two great big thick slices of Black Forest gateau and a gallon of dandelion and burdock lemonade. That's my favourite.'

'I've got a bit of chocolate in my pocket, but it's melted and stuck to the paper. Have you got anything?'

'Just a picture of John Wayne and a box of matches,' said Ewart. 'At least if we're still out here when it starts t' get dark we'll be able to light a fire.'

'To keep the wild animals away, I suppose.'

'It was the midgies I was thinking about. Forget the vultures, those things'll eat you alive, clothes and all.'

'We should get back to Rackwick,' I said.

'I know, but what about Francesco Alligator?'

'We could stay with your Uncle Gordon and then catch the first ferry tomorrow morning.'

'Does that mean we've got to walk back across the desert then down through that jungle of man-eating heather?'

'Unless you've got any better ideas.'

'This path. It leads down to the road, and the road leads back to Rackwick.'

I looked at the path and then down at the road, snaking its way between the massive hills. It was empty. We hadn't heard a car or seen anything vaguely suspicious since leaving Neville. We took the path. An hour later we were plodding along the road, about two miles from Rackwick Bay.

'I've decided what I'm going to do when I grow up,' said Ewart wearily.

'What's that?'

'I'm going to buy a bus, a big bus, and drive up and down this road, picking people up and giving them lifts for free.'

'Sounds like a waste of time to me.'

'How come?'

'No-one ever seems to use it.'

'Well, either that, or I might just fetch over a thousand bulldozers and flatten that stupid hill, with its stupid man-eating heather. Me legs feel like I've been paddling in a pool of piranhas.'

We turned a corner and stopped in our tracks. Up ahead was a motorbike and sidecar, parked by the side of the road. Someone was crouching down behind it, cursing every nut and bolt that held it together. They stood up, with a spanner in one hand and a black beret in the other. It was Elsie.

'Elsie!'

She was no more than thirty yards away, but we must have given her a scare, because she dropped her spanner on the road and then started fumbling about with her binocular case.

'Elsie . . . It's me . . . Stanley Buckle,' I panted, running towards her. 'And this is my friend . . . Ewart Gunn.'

I turned to introduce Ewart, but Ewart was where I'd left him, standing in the bend of the road.

'Stanley. Fancy meeting you here.'

'Yes,' I smiled.

'I told you we'd meet again. I had that feeling in my bones, remember?'

I nodded. Her hands and face were smeared with black oil. She folded her beret and mopped her brow.

'Whatever must I look like?' she said.

'What happened?' I asked, looking down at the motorbike.

'I'm afraid this machine and I are not getting on at all well. I hired it in Stromness from a very nice man, who assured me it went "like a bird". Those were his very words, "like a bird". Unfortunately the "bird" turned out to be a "lame duck". I brought it across on the ferry this morning and I've been limping round this island on it all day, trying to find some puffins and now, on my way back home, it's just stopped.

'There's plenty of fuel. Nothing's flooded. Plugs and points are all in good working order. I think it's possibly a blockage in the fuel pipe. I've just given that a clean and now I'm going to give it one more try.'

She sat astride the motorbike, turned the ignition key, bounced down on the kick-start and it spluttered into life. As she revved back on the throttle a cloud of smelly black smoke billowed out of the exhaust, covering her and the bike. I stepped back, coughing. She turned off the engine and the smoke drifted slowly away. She was staring at me with her downward-looking eyes.

'What's wrong, Stanley? I know there's *something* wrong. You can tell me.'

'You're not going to believe this.'

'Try me.'

So I told Elsie the whole story, just like I'd told Ewart and just like I'd told Neville. She listened in complete silence until I got to the bit where Francesco Allegretto shot at Neville through the window.

'Oh, you poor, *poor* boys. How absolutely *dreadful!*

Seeing your friend killed like that.'

'But Neville wasn't killed. The bullet missed.'

'Missed?'

'Yes. At exactly the same time as the hit-man pulled the trigger, Neville burnt himself with a lighted match. He dropped the matchbox and bent down quickly, trying to catch it. He must have missed the bullet by a millionth of a second. He's dead lucky.'

'Quite.'

'And Ewart and me were trying to catch the last ferry to Stromness so that we could tell the police, but we've missed it. So we're walking back to Rackwick Bay to stay with Ewart's Uncle Gordon, until the morning.'

'What a story!'

'It's not a story. It's true.'

'All the best stories *are* true, Stanley. Now tell me, is that where your Neville is now, safe with this Uncle Gordon?'

'No. He's hiding in an old croft up on the cliff at the other end of the bay.'

'I see. And does Ewart's uncle have a telephone?'

'Not unless he's found one on the beach,' muttered Ewart who'd just joined us.

'Pardon?'

'No, he hasn't and the phone box at Rackwick's dead. Francesco Allegretto's cut the line.'

'Well. It looks very much as if we're all stranded,' said Elsie, with surprising calmness. 'Stranded, but not defeated. Hop in, we're going back to Rackwick.'

'Me mam says that I'm not supposed to accept lifts from strangers,' said Ewart, staring down at his feet.

'Hardly a stranger! Stanley and I are travelling companions.'

'That's right,' I said.

'And, if you don't mind me saying so, you two boys look quite exhausted.'

'Suppose so,' muttered Ewart.

Ewart and I climbed into the sidecar. Elsie pulled a pair of goggles from her coat pocket and stretched them over her eyes. She turned the key and revved the engine loudly. Then, with her binocular case slung over her shoulder, she released the brake, let out the clutch and we all surged forwards, through a cloud of black smoke.

CHAPTER EIGHTEEN

Purple Haze

It was half past six. Rackwick Bay was deserted. Someone had left a bicycle propped against the telephone box. Elsie stopped the motorbike alongside it and looked around. Then, without saying a word, she drove up the hillside to The Eyrie, and Ewart jumped out. The family of white ducks were back on the turf roof, huddled round the chimney, but Uncle Gordon was nowhere to be seen.

'He'll be back soon,' said Ewart. 'He'll be down on the beach, maybes.'

Elsie pulled the goggles off her eyes and stretched them over her brow. 'I don't like it,' she said. 'I don't like it at all. First your friend Neville and now Ewart's Uncle Gordon.'

'What d'you mean?' asked Ewart, sounding worried.

'No-one's at home where they ought to be. There's a killer on the loose and everyone's wandering about the hillsides as if they were on a Sunday School picnic.'

'I think the hit-man's gone. I think he caught the last ferry,' I said.

'You might *think* he's gone, but do we *know* he's gone? In a situation like this, we'd do well to remember there is safety in numbers. We should all be sticking together. And that includes your friend Neville.'

When I thought about it, she was right. If Francesco Allegretto was still on the island and looking for Neville, he'd find him, sooner or later. And Neville on his own would be a sitting duck, but Neville with me, and Ewart, and Uncle Gordon, and now Elsie, that would be something else. Elsie was right. I felt like kicking myself. I'd come all this way to try and save Neville and then I'd left him to fend for himself. He wouldn't stand a chance. He was useless.

We drove to the far end of the bay, where the giant cliffs of The Sneuk rose four hundred feet into the air. They were like some massive ocean liner, bursting out from the hillside and crashing into the sea. It took some time to find the old sheep track Neville told us about and then a bit longer to persuade Ewart to climb up it, but Uncle Gordon wasn't on the beach and he didn't fancy being left alone, not after what Elsie had just said. It was a struggle, especially for Elsie. The heather was that thick, that every time you brushed against it there'd be clouds of purple pollen. Half the time you couldn't see where you were putting your feet and the other half you were tripping up and sliding backwards. I was in the lead, Elsie was right behind me and Ewart was at the back. We were getting near the top. The air was still and below us you could hear the surge of the waves. I stopped to get my breath.

'*Fermate Vi!* Do not move! Stay where you are!'

All three of us turned round. And there, no more than twenty yards behind us, standing in the heather, was Francesco Allegretto.

'Aw, no!' moaned Ewart.

Then everything seemed to go in slow motion. It was like watching it happen from a long way away. Like I was watching it on telly in the front room back home, with my mum and my little sister. I suppose, right at that moment, that's where I most wanted to be and I wanted it so badly that it felt as real as anything else.

Francesco Allegretto reached inside his jacket with

his left hand. Ewart dropped to his knees and covered his face. Elsie ducked down behind him and began rummaging in her battered binocular case. Francesco Allegretto still had his left hand inside his jacket. He was waving with his other arm, the one with the metal claw, like he wanted me to get out of the way. Then Elsie stood up from behind Ewart, pulled out a long black gun, and shot Francesco Allegretto. It was like he'd been on a piece of string and someone had yanked him backwards. One second he was there and the next he was gone. All that was left was a purple haze of pollen where he'd once stood.

There was hardly any noise. Just a loudish *phutt*. I looked down at the gun in Elsie's hand. A thin ribbon of grey smoke was curling upwards from the long black silencer. The air was still and below us you could hear the surge of the waves.

She turned round and pointed the barrel at my head.

'One scream,' she whispered, 'one word, and I will blow your little brains across this hillside. Do I make myself clear?'

I nodded. She needn't have worried. I was too scared to speak.

'Now! Both of you go in front. Do exactly as I say and you may live. Annoy me, and you will certainly die. Like that stupid policeman.'

We were like two zombies. One foot in front of the

other. Not daring to speak. Not even looking at each other. This was mad. It didn't make sense. Elsie Robinson couldn't be a hired killer. She had the same hairdo as my granny.

'Stop!' she ordered.

We'd just turned a corner and there was the old croft. It had a rusty tin roof with a hole at one end, where some bits had blown off. There were two small windows that were boarded up, and the door was hanging off its hinges, as if it had been forced open.

'You will walk up to the door, but not inside. You will stop beside that rock and you will ask Mr Windrush kindly to step outside. Do I make myself clear?'

I nodded.

'Now go. I am sure I do not need to remind you what will happen if you disobey me in any way.'

I started walking. Ewart followed me. I stopped at the rock and looked down. There was a small blue butterfly opening and closing its wings on the label of an empty whisky bottle. I looked up at the open door and opened my mouth, but nothing came out, just a sound like rusty hinges creaking in the wind. I couldn't breathe. I looked across at Ewart. His face was that pale that even the freckles had disappeared.

'I will count to five,' said Elsie Robinson, through gritted teeth. 'One. Two . . .'

'Neville!' shouted Ewart.

I stared at the door, willing him not to come out.

'Neville. It's us. Ewart and Stanley.'

But nobody came.

Elsie Robinson edged towards the door, with the gun held close to her chest. She stopped outside and listened, pressed against the stone wall. There wasn't a sound. Then suddenly she threw herself through the door, spinning round, holding the gun in both hands straight out in front of her. I was listening for the shots. I looked across at Ewart, but he didn't look back. There was a crash from inside the croft and a few seconds later Elsie Robinson stormed out. She slammed the door to one side, strode towards us and kicked the empty whisky bottle so that it smashed to pieces on the rock. She raised her right arm and pointed the gun at the sky, wagging it slowly like a long black finger, staring downwards and directly at us.

'Where . . . is . . . he?'

CHAPTER NINETEEN

Monday, Monday

It hit me like a ton of bricks. I'd got everything totally wrong. It was as if I'd done a jigsaw, where all the pieces fitted perfectly. Except my finished picture was completely different from the one on the front of the box.

Francesco Allegretto wasn't the hired killer, he was a *policeman*. At least, he had been a policeman until Elsie Robinson shot him dead in the heather. *Elsie Robinson* was the hired killer. My head was spinning, the same way it had earlier that morning when I'd looked over the edge of the cliff. I was trying to work out what had really happened.

I was watching myself in the cafe at King's Cross

151

station. I was watching Elsie Robinson looking at my photograph of Neville. I was watching myself leaning over the side of the St Ola, *holding on to her hand. And then I was staring into the eyes of Francesco Allegretto, except now they weren't sinister or menacing, they were worried and concerned. And I could hear him telling me, 'Choose your friends carefully'.*

And now it was all too late. I'd played right into the real killer's hands. I'd led her straight to Neville's hideout, and all she had to do was wait. It was only a matter of time before Neville returned. She pushed us both inside the old croft, then pulled the door to, so that it looked the same as when we'd arrived.

'Sit!' she snapped, pointing to an old iron bedstead, with a dirty grey mattress.

The croft was one long room, with a bare earth floor. There was a fireplace at one end and the bedstead at the other. There were no tables or chairs, just a couple of fish boxes and a length of rope stretched between the walls that somebody, sometime or other, must have used to hang their clothes on. On one of the fishing boxes was Neville's paint-spattered rucksack with a bottle of Tio Pepe sticking out of the top.

Ewart and I sat down on the bed. It was dark in there, except for over by the fireplace, where there was still a bit of sunlight shining through the hole in the roof. It sliced through the shadows and lit a patch

152

of bright green moss. Elsie turned her back to us and walked towards the fireplace until she stood in the spotlight.

'It is regrettable that I lost my temper. I tried to spare your lives. That was a mistake. I should have shot you both alongside your friend, Mr Windrush, then there would be none of this untidiness. I cannot bare untidiness. It gives me a headache and makes me irritable. But do not concern yourselves, I intend to rectify my mistake.'

'I want me mam,' whimpered Ewart.

'Too late for that!' laughed Elsie. 'You ought to have heeded her advice about not accepting lifts from strangers. A boy should always obey his mother.'

For the first time, it was really sinking in that we were way out of our depth, that we might die, and *not* in our sleep. I looked down at my feet, thinking about about *my* mum . . . and my dad . . . and my little sister. On the floor there was a candle, a tin of tobacco and a piece of paper. The piece of paper had writing on it. I twisted my head round so that I could read the writing.

'What are you looking at?' demanded Elsie.

'Nothing.'

'You do not twist your head round like an owl to look at nothing.'

'It's just a piece of paper.'

'Bring it here!'

I walked across and gave her the piece of paper.

'What does this mean? "MONDAY 7PM. FORGOT VINCENT. BACK SOON. NEVILLE." Who is this Vincent?'

'His cat,' I said.

Elsie looked at me long and hard. The eyes were burning holes in my skull. She could tell I wasn't lying.

'So Mr Windrush has a cat,' she said thoughtfully. 'He must be very fond of this cat to risk his life like this. Very fond and very foolish. Personally, I have always found that cats are perfectly capable of taking care of themselves. They have little need of human company.'

'Vincent's hurt his paw,' I said.

Elsie frowned and looked down at the ground. 'That's a shame,' she said. 'Now I understand. We will sit patiently and await Mr Windrush's return.'

We waited for what seemed like hours. The inside of the croft grew darker and the spotlight of sun faded until the bright green moss was swallowed up in black shadow. Through the window I could see a coppery pink edge to the clouds. The sun was beginning to set.

Elsie kept going over to the door and peering out the crack. She was getting impatient. She kept pacing round and round the bare earth floor, like a bee searching for a soft spot into which to place her sting.

It was cold and Ewart was shivering. I didn't know what had happened to Neville and I wasn't sure that I cared any more. I was too scared.

Suddenly Elsie grabbed the rope that was stretched between the walls and yanked it down, then she pulled a knife out of her pocket and cut it in two.

'Here! You! Stanley Buckle. Tie your friend to the bedstead with his hands behind his back.'

I took a length of rope and did what she asked, trying not to look at the barrel of the gun which was pointing towards us.

'Make sure it is tight,' she said. 'If it isn't, I will shoot you.'

I pulled the knots tight.

'Now. Back to back.'

I knelt down on the floor with my back to Ewart. I could feel him trembling.

'Hands behind your back!' she snapped.

She put the gun on the floor and tied my hands to the bedstead alongside Ewart's. Then she picked up the gun and walked to the door, kicking it open with her foot.

'It appears that Mr Windrush is having trouble finding his cat. I must go and help him. Make yourselves comfortable. Later we will take a walk together – along the cliff top.'

CHAPTER TWENTY

Fire!

'Has she gone?' whispered Ewart.

'I think so.'

'She means it, doesn't she?'

'I think so.'

'It's her eyes. Have you seen her eyes?'

'Yes.'

'They're killer's eyes. They've gone like that from all the evil she's done.'

'She's kind to small animals.'

'I'm a small animal and she's not very kind to me! She's going to kill us, Stanley. She's not pretending. She's going to come back after she's killed Neville and she's going to push us off the cliff.

And, I don't know about you, but I can't fly.'

I didn't know what to say.

'I can't believe this is really happening,' continued Ewart. 'It's worse than anything I've ever imagined. I want it to stop, but it won't, it just keeps on going. I want to be able to switch it off, like the telly. Or I want someone like John Wayne to walk in and save us.'

I sat in the dark imagining John Wayne riding up the hillside pursued by Elsie Robinson on her motorbike. He wasn't scared. He had a rifle in one hand, a fag in his mouth, and a box of matches in his other hand.

'Ewart?'

'I'm still here.'

'Have you still got that box of matches in your pocket?'

'Yes. Why?'

'You know that trick you do with matches, striking them with one hand like John Wayne?'

'Yes.'

'Do you think you could do it with your hands tied behind your back?'

'Maybes.'

''Cause, if you could, then you could burn the rope round my wrists and we could get free.'

'Great, but I can't get my hand in my pocket.'

'I think I can, if you twist round a bit.'

Ewart twisted round and I managed to stretch my fingertips into his pocket and pull out the box

157

of matches. I placed them in his hands.

'I can't see what I'm doing. Even John Wayne gets t'see what he's doing.'

'Just pretend it's pitch-black and the matches are in the back of your saddlebag and the Apaches are hot on your heels and you're desperate for a fag.'

'But I don't smoke. Smoking's bad for your health.'

'So's being pushed off cliffs.'

'I'll have a go.'

I held my breath and stared straight ahead at the wall. I could barely make out the different stones. There was a lot of fumbling about behind me, then a faint *crackling* and the stones came alive in an orange glow as our shadows danced across them, up and over, disappearing into the blackness of the roof.

'I'm scared I'll burn your skin,' said Ewart.

'You'll burn your own skin if you don't hurry up.'

'Tell us if it hurts.'

'Don't worry.' *AAAAAAAARGH!*

It hurt. And it kept on hurting. I remembered that when John Wayne had an arrow pulled out of him in *The Alamo* he was given a 'slug of Ol'Red Eye' and a piece of rawhide to bite down on. All I could do was grit my teeth and watch the shadows until, after six matches and six minor burns, Ewart got the hang of it and we could smell the sweet smell of burning rope and hear the music of its sizzle.

I was free. With the last match I lit the candle and

untied Ewart. My wrists were stinging like mad, but it didn't matter. All that mattered was that we got out of there and got away before Elsie came back. We stepped outside and looked around. Nobody. The sun had set. There was just a smudge of orange left on the horizon. The hills were purply-black and the cliffs were the colour of dried blood.

'How long d'you think she's been gone?' whispered Ewart, looking down the hillside into the darkness.

'Not sure. Ten, fifteen minutes?'

'She'll be down on the beach then.'

'How long will it take her to get up to Neville's place?' I asked.

'She's not that fast and if she's walking along the beach the boulders'll slow her down. Then she's got that hill to climb. Maybe another thirty minutes, maybes longer.'

'Is there a short cut?'

'If you stay high and loop round the bay you could be at Neville's in fifteen minutes, but that's in the daylight.'

'That means we could still get to Neville first and warn him.'

'Are you crazy?'

'No. There's still time. We've got to get going.'

'*You* get going if you're daft enough. Forget the "we". I'm heading straight for Uncle Gordon's. I can see the light from here. And when I get there I'm bolting the door and hammering a plank across with six-inch nails. If you've got any sense, you'll be standing behind me.'

'What about Neville?'

'Stuff Neville! It's his lookout. He got himself into this mess. He said so himself. I'm not getting killed just 'cause he's a greedy sod that wants to be famous.'

All of a sudden I felt like I was back, standing on the edge of that gaping blackness I'd seen when I was little. Ewart was pulling me one way and the blackness was pulling the other. Only this time the person in the blackness wasn't dead. Not yet, anyway.

'Are you coming then?' asked Ewart.

'No.'

'I'll see you then . . . Maybes.'

CHAPTER TWENTY-ONE

Paint it Black

When Ewart left I felt more alone than ever, but I didn't blame him. In a way he was right. For him, Neville was just this old weirdo painting crazy paintings, who'd made him a cup of tea. Whereas, to me, Neville had been like a dad. Ewart had a chance to go, and he'd gone. I had that chance too, but I was staying. I'd come too far to turn back.

I watched Ewart's silhouette until all there was just blackness and a rustling of heather, then I turned and started running across the top of the hill. Every now and then the moon would peer through the clouds and I'd get a chance to check my bearings.

After about twenty minutes I was standing on the

far hill, looking down on the roof of The Crow's Nest. The moon was hidden behind a bank of cloud. There were just a few stars. It was very quiet. I was listening to my breathing. Concentrating. Listening . . . Listening to someone else's breathing! Someone was crouching in the darkness behind me.

'Puss puss puss puss puss.'

'Neville?'

'Oh my God!' he gasped, 'Don't do that, Stanley. That's the second, no, the *third* time today I've almost had a heart attack. What are you doing here anyway? Where's Ewart? Where's Francesco Alligator, or whatever he calls himself? And why are we whispering?'

'Francesco Allegretto's dead.'

'That's good, isn't it?'

'Francesco Allegretto was a policeman.'

'*WHAT?* That's bad.'

'Did I ever mention Elsie Robinson?'

'I can't remember.'

'Elsie's the hired killer.'

'You're making this up, aren't you?'

'No. I'm not. Honest. I know it's a bit confusing . . .'

'*Confusing?*'

'SSSSSSHHHHHHHH! Keep your voice down. She's out there now.'

Just then the heather behind us began to rustle.

'Mmmmmeeeeooooowwwwww.'

162

'Vincent,' sighed Neville, 'what a relief. Where've you been? I've been scouring this hillside for hours. Hold this, Stanley.' And he reached behind him and produced a wicker travelling basket. 'Now, let's be a good pussy. Let's not give daddy any trouble. We're all going on a little walkies, but first we'll have some nice juicy sardines.'

He took a tin of sardines out of his pocket, opened it and placed it inside the wicker basket at the back. Vincent sniffed the air, climbed inside and Neville shut the lid. He was just going to say something, but stopped.

Below us a beam of light was probing the hillside. For a brief moment it settled on the door of The Crow's Nest then it went out.

'Elsie?' mouthed Neville, pointing down the hill-side. I didn't need to say anything. He could tell from the expression on my face that I was scared stiff. We crouched in silence.

Below us, in the darkness, somebody was moving. Whoever it was had reached the flat bit of grass in front of Neville's door. The moon blinked through the clouds and shone down on the tight silver curls. She walked towards the door. It was closed. Everything seemed to hold its breath. The light breeze that was ruffling the heather dropped to a whisper and even the moon shrank back again, behind the clouds.

Then she struck. With one massive kick the door

burst open and she darted inside, *phutt, phutt, phutt*.

'I don't think she likes the paintings,' muttered Neville. But I could tell he was scared.

Inside The Crow's Nest the beam of the torch flashed backwards and forwards like an angry wasp caught in a jam jar. There was the *crash* of breaking glass and what sounded like a chair being smashed against the wall.

'We've got to get out of here,' I said.

'I *know*, but where to?'

I looked around. Uphill was too steep, where I'd come from was too exposed, and downhill was suicide. There wasn't much choice. I pointed to a track through the heather behind Neville.

'Where's that go?'

'It joins up with the path to the Old Man.'

'You go in front,' I said.

Neville picked up Vincent and set off. I followed close behind. We were as quiet as mice, until Neville tripped and dropped the basket.

'*MMMMMMMEEEEEOOOOOWWWWWW!*'

The blackness round about suddenly turned dark green. I looked over my shoulder and stared into the white eye of the torch.

'*Run!*' I shouted.

But Neville was already charging through the heather with Vincent's basket clamped to his chest. I don't remember hearing any shots. All I remember is running and stumbling in the darkness until the narrow track across the hillside joined the bigger path, the same one we'd taken earlier that day. I kept looking back, but couldn't see anybody following us. Even so, we didn't slow down. It was strange. The peat was that soft we couldn't hear our own footsteps, and the black was bottomless. It seemed to swallow everything up, even rocks. The only clue we had where to put our feet was the odd glimmer of white quartz embedded in a rock or a stone.

We must have been half-walking, half-running, for almost an hour when we reached the Old Man. 'He' was tilting slightly backwards, looking even shakier in the dark than he had in the light. We were standing near the edge of the cliff, where earlier that same day I'd looked down and seen Neville painting.

'Stop a bit,' panted Neville, 'I've got t'get . . . m'breath back . . . s'no use . . . I'll have t'give up . . . smoking . . . Oh no! . . . Look!'

I looked over my shoulder and saw the beam of a torch tracing the line of the path, no more than twenty minutes behind us.

'It's her, isn't it?' said Neville.

'Probably,' I whispered, 'but maybe . . . maybe it's someone else, like Uncle Gordon. Maybe Elsie gave up and left and maybe Uncle Gordon's come looking for us.'

Neville was silent. We were both staring at the

speck of white that was steadily weaving its way though the blackness, getting closer and closer.

'Gordon would have shouted,' said Neville. 'This one's too quiet to be friendly.'

'What're we going to do?'

'I don't know. I can't run any further. This cat weighs a ton.'

'Maybe you should let Vincent go.'

'You're right,' said Neville putting down the wicker basket. 'I was worried about his paw, but he stands a better chance on his own. Cats can look after themselves.' Then he undid the leather strap and opened the lid.

'Come on, tiger. You're free. Off you go.'

But Vincent wouldn't budge. He'd dug his claws into the wickerwork and was pressing himself into a corner, *yowling* indignantly. I looked back over my shoulder.

'She's getting closer,' I croaked.

'*Vincent!* For goodness' sake,' pleaded Neville, putting his hand in the basket. This provoked a particularly vicious *yowl* and Neville pulled his hand quickly out, but not quickly enough. He stared at the three parallel tracks of blood in disbelief.

'He's never done that before.'

'Neville, we're not going to be able to get away.'

'I can't just leave Vincent for that mad woman.'

'I think she quite likes cats.'

Neville looked down at the basket, then across at the torch.

'She's almost here!' I cried.

'We'll have to hide. Quick! Follow me!' said Neville, stepping over the edge of the cliff.

'We can't go down there in the dark. We'll kill ourselves.'

'We might, and we might not, but if we hang around here *she* certainly will.'

We stood together at the top of the steep path that led down to the grassy ledge. There was a cold wind blowing back up the cliff from the sea and the dark 'wrinkles' of the Old Man were crammed with the soft white shapes of hundreds and hundreds of sleeping gulls.

'I'll go first,' said Neville. 'It looks worse than it is. Goodbye, Vincent.'

I took a final glance over my shoulder. Vincent was still cowering inside the wicker basket. The white eye of the torch was getting bigger. It couldn't have been more than five minutes away. There was no alternative. I let Neville get ahead then I followed, feeling my way with my hands, listening to Neville grunting and groaning below me. Slipping and sliding but somehow staying upright, until I was there beside him on the grass ledge.

'This way!' whispered Neville, following a narrow path round a corner and behind a large rock.

'*Sssssh!* Let's wait and see what she does. We might lose her.'

We waited, peering out from behind the rock, back up the steep path to the edge of the cliff, two hundred feet or so above our heads. When the torchlight didn't appear straightaway I began thinking we'd lost her. But I was wrong. The edge of the cliff suddenly turned brilliant purple, as the beam of the torch touched the heather. It was like watching an artist paint on a black canvas. The beam of light was the brush. There was this single stroke of brilliant purple and then the 'brush' moved down to a big blob of green and began spreading it backwards and forwards until it found little smudges of red and orange, where Neville had mixed his paint on the rocks. Even then we thought she might have lost us, because the torchlight disappeared and everything returned to black, but half a minute later a tiny golden rectangle appeared on the purple edge.

'Oh no!' muttered Neville.

There was a faint crunching sound and the wicker basket flew up then down into the gull-filled chasm, smashing to pieces on the rocks below. Neville's face seemed to crumple with emotion.

'*Why?*'

The white eye of the torch left the purple edge and began to follow us down the steep path.

'It's all the way down to the bottom then,' said

Neville, swallowing back some tears. 'We've no other choice. There's a path of sorts. I've been down once. But that was in daylight.'

'Neville, I'm sorry.'

'It's not your fault. It's my fault. I should have left him at The Crow's Nest. I was just lonely and wanted the company. And now . . .' He peered over the edge, but you could only *hear* the waves – the waves and the wind.

'Stick right behind me,' he said, grabbing my shoulder. 'Try and watch where I put my feet. And *don't* look down!'

'It doesn't make much difference,' I said, staring into the blackness.

'No. I suppose not.'

I concentrated as hard as I could. I knew that I couldn't afford to let my mind wander, because every time it did start to wander I'd see myself falling through space, somersaulting over and over, like the wicker basket. And once you start imagining something like that in that kind of situation it's only a matter of time before it's really happening.

I thought about my feet, and where I was putting them. And I thought about the seagulls perched on the tiny ledges of the Old Man, and the puffins nesting in the old rabbit burrows on the edge of the cliff. And gradually the sound of the waves grew louder and louder until we were standing at the bottom in the double-decker graveyard of massive stone blocks that led out to the foot of the Old Man. We both turned at the same time and looked back up the path. The torchlight was now crossing the grassy ledge.

'She doesn't give up, does she?' muttered Neville. 'I must be worth more than I thought!'

'I don't think it's just the money.'

'What else?'

'Professional pride. She's supposed to be the best there is.'

'That's all we need, a "hit-lady" with a reputation to consider!'

We looked around. The tide was high, beating against the base of the cliffs, cutting off any chance of escape along the coast. It seemed hopeless. We'd reached a dead end. We were trapped.

CHAPTER TWENTY-TWO

Meet on the Ledge

'What are they?'

'What are what?'

'Those thin black lines. They're like ropes hanging down from higher up the Old Man.'

'They are ropes!' said Neville. 'They must have been left behind by those crazy people that were climbing it for television . . . It's funny that.'

'What?'

'Funny to think that just a couple of weeks ago there were millions of eyes, glued to the screen, watching this place.'

'I wish someone was watching now.'

'Maybe they are.'

We were both quiet for a time, watching the ropes swaying silently in the night. Then Neville turned towards me with some serious frown lines creasing his brow.

'Are you thinking what I'm thinking?'

'I *think* I am.'

'Have you ever . . . ?'

'No. Never. Just trees.'

'Me neither. Just stairs.'

It took longer than I expected to scramble over the massive stone blocks. The moonlight seemed to smudge all the details and the shadows were as black as peat. Every now and then, one of them would wobble when you stood on it. As we got closer the Old Man seemed to grow bigger, like he'd suddenly stood up. He was mostly straight up and down or overhanging, but the bottom hundred feet of the south face, which is where the ropes were hanging down from, leant back a bit. It was steep, but it wasn't vertical. By the time Neville arrived at the bottom I'd already grabbed the end of one of the ropes.

'What d'you think?' he asked, squinting upwards.

'I think I can reach that ledge,' I said, pointing up.

'It's an awful long way off the ground.'

'We haven't got much choice. The only alternative's to play hide-and-seek amongst these boulders. And she's got a torch.'

'*And* a gun.'

'Exactly.'

'I don't know. It just seems like suicide trying to climb this thing at night.'

'It's suicide not to. There's no way back. We've got to go up. It's the one place she won't be able to follow us.'

'What'll you do? Pull yourself up?'

'Suppose so,' I said, pulling hard on the rope. And as I pulled the end of the other rope rose into the air.

'That's a bit of luck, they're joined,' said Neville. 'They must be looped round something higher up. It means you can tie yourself onto the end of one rope while I pull on the other. That way, if you fall off, I'll have got you. Safe as houses.'

I wanted to believe him, but I knew the houses he was talking about were scheduled for demolition. The first ten feet were easy, like walking up steep stairs. The next ten feet were a bit harder and then suddenly I was high. I looked down at my feet and beyond them to Neville's anxious face and then back up and across at the flickering torchlight, which was making slow but steady progress down the path towards the bridge of rubble. I felt a tug on the rope round my waist, gritted my teeth, and carried on.

There was barely any moonlight. I had to grope my way up, trying to 'read' the rock the way a blind person reads Braille. 'Looking' with my fingertips, stroking its smoothness until they sank into a sharp incut, then pulling up and pushing up, and trusting and searching. And all the time the Old Man was 'breathing' with the sighing of the waves and the whistling of the wind, willing me on, inch by inch, foot by foot, hold by hold, letting me balance and rest and stretch and pull, until I was there on the ledge. It wasn't much bigger than the average bed, but it felt the size of a football pitch.

I wanted to shout, but kept quiet in case it alerted Elsie Robinson. Instead I quickly pulled in the slack rope, coiling it onto the ledge. The wind was blowing from the land which must have carried most of the sound out to sea, but even so I was sure she'd spotted us. I leant over the edge, looking down, keeping the rope as tight as I possibly could, hoping it would hurry Neville up and all the time the torchlight was moving closer and closer.

Neville was only ten, or maybe fifteen, feet below me when the torch stopped moving and she fired the first shot. There was a kind of *tzingg* then a crack as the bullet bit into the rock halfway between me and him, scattering a small cloud of dust.

'Hurry up!' I shouted.

He muttered something under his breath and kept climbing. There as another *tzingg* and a crack as a second bullet hit something softer. *'Are you all right?'*

'That's the daftest question I've heard. How can I

possibly be all right dangling from a rope in the middle of the night with a psychopathic granny after me? What's all this dust?'

Neville hadn't realized.

'Come on!' And I yanked the rope as he hauled himself onto the ledge like a beached whale.

'Quickly! Behind this rock.'

He started to lift himself up.

'KEEP DOWN!'

'OK. OK. Keep your hair on!' he said, as another bullet *tzingged* through the air, taking with it a sizable chunk of rock. *'She's shooting at us!'*

'Behind here. QUICK!'

Neville scrambled to the back of the ledge, joining me behind a shield of a protruding rock that was three feet thick. We dragged the rope after us then dug in our heels and pressed our backs against the rock. There was no way that Elsie Robinson could follow us, shoot at us, or even *see* us, from down below. We were one hundred feet above a swirling sea with a clear sky, a light breeze and a zillion twinkling stars. We were cold and tired and hungry, but we were alive. Elsie Robinson had missed her chance.

I started crying. I couldn't help it. I suppose it was partly to do with Vincent and partly to do with all the tension that had built up so much inside that it had to come out. Pretty soon Neville was crying too. We sat there, clinging to each other, like a pair

175

of overgrown seagulls on a nest of coiled ropes.

'Here, take my jumper,' sniffed Neville from somewhere inside it as he pulled it over his head. 'By the way, whatever happened to Ewart?'

'He's with his Uncle Gordon. I expect they'll come looking for us in the morning.'

'That's a relief. I mean, it's a relief that he's safe with Gordon. Nice lad Ewart.'

'Yes.'

'Oh! I'd give my left arm for a fag right now.'

'What about your right?'

'I need that for painting . . . Never thought to bring any baccy. I wasn't expecting such an excursion. I left it in that old croft up the hill.'

'Best place for it.'

'You're right. It's a bad habit, stunts your growth and shortens your life. And there's enough people trying to do that for me as it is.'

I nodded then yawned and let my head sink inside the warm folds of Neville's old brown jumper until just my eyes and the top of my head were poking out. It smelled a bit of cigarette smoke, but mostly it smelled of oil paint. We were quiet for a bit.

'So you never told me,' he said.

'Told you what?'

'What you thought about the new paintings.'

'You mean the ones you've been doing up here on Hoy?'

'Yes.'

'I think they're good, *really good*. They're the best I've seen you do.'

'You're not just saying that to cheer me up?'

'No. Why would I bother? They're selling for millions anyway. They're queuing round the block down in London. You're famous. What d'you need to know what I think for?'

'Because you tell the truth.'

'What about the people that buy them? Don't they tell the truth?'

'Some of them. Some of them'll buy my paintings because they really like them, but there's others'll buy them just because I'm famous.'

'But, so long as they buy them, that's what counts. It doesn't really matter *why*, does it?'

'Yes, it does. People really liking what I do is more important than the money. And, in the end, the *most* important thing – possibly the only really important thing – is that *I* like what I do.'

'So why d'you want to be famous in the first place?'

'Immortality, I suppose.'

'That's funny.'

'What?'

'You wanting to be famous for the immortality and it's because you've become famous that everyone's trying to kill you.'

'Not *everyone*.'

'But you'd rather be dead and remembered, than alive and forgotten about.'

'Well, if you put it like that . . . No. I'd much rather be alive to enjoy being famous, but maybe that's asking too much. What d'you think?'

'I don't see why. Not if you're good enough.'

'You're right,' he said and sat for a while in silence. 'Tell me, is there any one painting that you like better than the others?'

I thought for a bit.

'I didn't really get a good look at the others in the studio, but I liked the one you finished this morning. I was looking at it when we were walking back to your house, The Crow's Nest, when it was strapped to the back of your rucksack. I think it's the best one you've ever done.'

'It's got a hole in it now.'

'Doesn't matter.'

'It's yours then.'

'You're kidding.'

'I'm not. If we ever get off this lump of rock and back home in one piece, it's yours. I'm giving it to you.'

The night wore on and we watched the stars drift slowly across the sky. We heard seals singing and snipe drumming and a breathtaking *whoosh* out at sea that may, or may not, have been a whale.

Neville talked about Vincent and I talked about my dad and all of the things that we used to do together before he died. And I told Neville about how my mum would start crying sometimes because I'd do something a certain way. Just a little thing, like scratching the side of my head, but the way I'd do it would remind her of him. Somehow it's those little things that survive. Peculiar little habits that say more about who you are and where you're from than any amount of teeth or fingerprints. Neville listened. Then, after what must have been hours and hours, the sky in the east began to lighten and across from where we sat the cliffs of the headland began to crawl out of the darkness.

'Don't you just *love* this place,' sighed Neville.

I didn't reply. I was thinking about something else.

'Neville?'

'Yes.'

'When did you first come to the Orkneys?'

'Oh, let me see. It must have been ten . . . eleven . . . years ago. I'd just finished at art college and I came out here with a tent and some paints and a head full of bright ideas. It was the best eight weeks of my life.'

'So why did you wait so long to come back?'

Neville looked up at the few remaining stars and took a deep breath.

'I met a girl . . . here on Hoy. She was on her own,

doing the same kind of thing I was, getting away from everything and everyone, except she hadn't come quite so far. She lived on the main island of Orkney. Her father was a minister over there. There was just the two of us, swimming and painting and walking the hills by day and then at night, the camp-fires, the stars and . . . all the rest.

'When the eight weeks were over we decided to run away together and get married. We were crazy about each other. We went back to the main island. She was going to go home and get a few extra things and then we were going to sail away into the sunset. I wanted to go with her, but she thought it would be best to go alone. So I waited for her on the cobbled square in front of the harbour at Stromness. I waited and waited and all the time I was thinking, *Am I doing the right thing? Artists are supposed to suffer for their art. They're supposed to sacrifice every-thing in order to become famous. They shouldn't be tied down.*

'The time came for the *St Ola* to sail and she hadn't come back and, like a fool, I jumped on board and sailed away. And there hasn't been a single day, when I haven't regretted that decision. I can still see her now. I've never forgotten her. Those green eyes the colour of the sea. We used to joke that we were made for each other, that we'd found Paradise. I was her Adam and she was my . . .'

'Mr Windrush!' came a voice from way above our heads. 'I am pleased to make your acquaintance at last.'

We both looked up, up to the edge of the headland, three hundred feet above the waves and two hundred feet above our heads. Silhouetted against the pale pink dawn was the short, broad figure of Elsie Robinson. I felt the blood drain from my head.

'Your companion, Stanley Buckle, I have already met. Like a cat, he seems to have more than one life. In two minutes time the sun will rise and I will be able to see you both with perfect clarity. When that happens I am going to kill you. There is nowhere for you to hide, unless of course, you decide to jump.' And she began to laugh.

'Oh my God! Stanley. She's right. This is it. *This is really it!*'

The breeze had dropped and the air was completely still, as if the Old Man himself was holding his breath. I couldn't speak. I was trembling and staring with horror as she knelt down and slowly began unpacking the contents of her battered binocular case. All around us the sleeping gulls were waking up.

'Mrs Robinson!' shouted Neville, over the squawking of the gulls.

'Yes, Mr Windrush?'

'The boy . . . Stanley. He's got nothing to do with

this. Do whatever you have to do to me, but not the boy. He's innocent!'

'On the contrary, Mr Windrush. Stanley Buckle is *guilty*. He is guilty of being a nuisance.'

'But you can't shoot someone for being a nuisance!'

'Oh, but I can, Mr Windrush. I am going to shoot you, because that is what I have been paid to do and once I accept a contract I *never* give up. I am going to shoot Stanley Buckle because I *want* to!'

And as the words left her mouth the sun peered over the headland so that its brilliant scarlet rim framed the heather at her feet. And for a split-second it looked as though Elsie Robinson was standing in flames. She raised the gun above her head and then slowly and smoothly lowered it, until it was pointing directly at us. The Old Man flushed red in the rising sun.

'You've already killed my cat!' shouted Neville.

'I'm sorry? What?' she said, lowering the gun and stepping forward.

'My *cat*,' shouted Neville. 'You murdered my cat!'

But Elsie Robinson didn't reply; she was too busy scratching at her face and slapping at the air around her head.

'Midgies,' whispered Neville.

And we both watched, spellbound, as she tried to take aim again but began twitching and flapping as the midgies bit her face, until it looked almost as if she was *dancing* . . . dancing near the edge of the cliff where the puffins had made their nests in the deserted rabbit burrows and, as Uncle Gordon pointed out, had done such a thorough job of digging them out that it was a honeycomb waiting to crack.

And it cracked.

I think I remember her begin to scream, but then Neville smothered me in his arms and the gulls, who had been so rudely awakened, rose in deafening protest to fill the chasm with a screaming blizzard of indignation.

CHAPTER TWENTY-THREE

Good Day, Sunshine

About half an hour later another figure appeared on the cliff top wearing orange rubber gloves and carrying an ancient shotgun.

'If it's not a daft question, what're you both doing sitting up there?'

'*Gordon!*' shouted Neville.

'And what's happened to that nasty piece of work that's been going round scaring the livin' daylights out of small boys?'

'You mean Elsie?'

'Aye, that's her.'

'She's dead. She fell off the cliff.'

Uncle Gordon examined the giant bite-shaped scar on the edge of the cliff.

'Puffins,' he said. 'Just as well. I'm not too sure this thing works anyway. I found it on the beach last winter. I've got an old box of shells from the war, but I've been too scared to try them out.'

'Best unload it then,' suggested Neville.

'Never had them in,' said Uncle Gordon, fumbling around in his duffel-coat pocket. 'I think I dropped them on the way here.'

'If it's not a daft question, Gordon, why are you wearing rubber gloves?'

'Fingerprints.'

The sound of gulls filled the space between us and drowned our laughter. For a while Uncle Gordon was lost behind a snowstorm of feathers. When he reappeared it was without the rubber gloves.

'You're both in one piece then?'

'Yes.'

'Right then. I'll be off.'

'Hang on!' shouted Neville. 'What about us? How do we get down?'

'How did you get up?'

'We climbed, but . . .'

'Sit tight!' laughed Uncle Gordon, 'Ewart's away over the hill with that Italian policeman. They'll be phoning for a helicopter. I'll be away to get the breakfast on. I dare say you'll be peckish after your wee adventure.'

Three hours later we were sitting in the back garden of The Eyrie, surrounded by nearly one hundred orange rubber gloves, mostly left-hands. Uncle Gordon had set up a makeshift table and those without chairs made do with up-turned fishing boxes. There were nine of us altogether: myself and Neville, Gordon and Ewart, the four-man crew of the helicopter, and Captain Francesco Allegretto of Interpol.

Francesco Allegretto had come back from the 'dead' four or five hours after we'd seen him disappear in a purple haze. In fact, he'd never been dead, just unconscious. The bullet fired from Elsie Robinson's gun had missed his heart and hit the metal of his false right arm. The impact of it had knocked him off balance and he'd fallen back into the thick heather hitting his head on a large stone.

When he came round he'd staggered down to the beach and seen a light on in The Eyrie. Uncle Gordon had just finished grinding up some of his beach-combed coffee beans, and he'd put an Italian opera record on the old gramophone. Captain Allegretto thought he'd died and gone to heaven. Ewart thought he was dead anyway and told Uncle Gordon there was a ghost outside. Uncle Gordon let him in, gave him a cup of coffee, then bandaged his head.

He explained how he'd come to London from Milan on the trail of the notorious 'Black Widow', a female assassin with an awesome reputation. The 'Black Widow', alias Elsie Robinson, was on the 'most wanted' lists of almost every country in Europe. Captain Allegretto had followed her to the Orkneys, unaware of the contract that Patrick Fitzwilliam had taken out on Neville. He guessed there was more to Elsie Robinson's Orkney trip than bird-watching and tried to warn me on the train, without letting on who he was and why he was there. But when he discovered the telephone line had been cut at Rackwick Bay, then saw her climbing up the hillside with Ewart and me, he knew we were in great danger. He tried to stop us, but then things went badly wrong.

After breakfast the helicopter crew flew us to the hospital on the main island, near Stromness. Captain Allegretto needed his head seeing to and Neville, Ewart and I had to be checked over as well. Uncle Gordon came along to save a fare on the ferry and to buy some essentials he couldn't find on the beach.

Ewart had been quiet at breakfast. He'd spent most of the time looking down at the floor, but when the helicopter took off he opened up.

'*Wow!* It's fantastic, isn't it? It's even better than I

imagined. That's what I'm goin' to be when I'm bigger.'

'A helicopter pilot?'

'No, an astronaut! Imagine if this thing just kept going up and up and everything got smaller and smaller until you could see the whole world.'

'You're mad.'

'I'm sorry,' he said quietly.

'What for?'

'For running away last night. You won't tell anyone, will you?'

'No. Why should I? I'd have done the same if I'd been you.'

'Would you?'

'What did you tell your Uncle Gordon?'

'I told him what happened, but he didn't believe me. Not until Captain Alligator, there, banged on the door with his claw.'

'Did you tell *him* you'd run off?'

'Not *exactly*. I said we'd got split up. It sounded better.'

The hospital was new. The whole place had been painted pale green. It was meant to calm you down, and it might have, if the front door hadn't kept going *phut* every time it opened or closed. One nurse came and took Captain Allegretto off to the X-ray Department and another came and took Neville,

188

Ewart and me somewhere else. We each had to take our clothes off in a little cubicle with a pale green curtain drawn across. Then this lady doctor came and gave us the once-over. There was a policewoman there too. Her eyes nearly popped out of her head when I told the doctor how I got the burns on my wrists. The doctor said I should be more careful, drink lots of liquid and get some sleep. She put some cream on, then wrapped both wrists in white bandage. Ewart had sticking plasters all over his legs where the heather had cut them and Neville had a bandaged hand where Vincent had clawed it. We looked worse than when we went in.

When we were fixed up, we followed the policewoman back along the corridor and she showed us into a small square room with a pale green carpet and pale green plastic chairs. We sat listening to a pneumatic drill rattling at some tarmac outside, while two detectives from Stromness shuffled a lot of papers about and got ready to ask us some awkward questions.

I suppose we were all thinking our own thoughts. Neville must have been thinking about Vincent, or wondering how many years he was going to get for letting people think he was dead and wasting valuable police time. Ewart must have been wondering what his mum was going to say. And I was wondering if it was against the law not to tell the police when you *thought* there was going to be a crime committed, even though you *knew* they wouldn't believe you. I was just beginning to get worried when in walked Captain Allegretto with a smart new bandage on his head.

One flash of his Interpol ID card did the trick. The 'Black Widow' was missing, presumed dead. Nothing else seemed important. The only major downer was that the police insisted my mum was informed of my real whereabouts. She took it quite well at first, but I think that was shock. She'd thought I was safely bird-spotting in the Cairngorms, when all the time I'd been dicing with death in the Orkneys. It took a while to sink in and then there was no stopping her. Captain Allegretto did his best to calm her down by singing my praises, but it's hard to sing anything when you're holding the phone half a metre from your ear. Finally he gave up, shrugged his shoulders, tugged at his moustache, and said he'd escort me home personally. I was grateful for that.

CHAPTER TWENTY-FOUR

Something

By midday, we'd finished. No more questions. We were free to go. We all walked down to the harbour and Neville, Francesco and I bought tickets for the half past two ferry sailing back to the mainland. Uncle Gordon met us at the bottom of the main street with two carrier bags full of shopping.

'Well, if it isn't the "walking wounded"!'

Small crowds were gathering on either side of the narrow street, looking and pointing, like they were expecting something to happen. Word had got round about last night's battle on the Isle of Hoy and there wasn't much doubt about who was the hero. People kept coming up to Neville, asking him if he was the *famous* Neville Windrush then shaking his good hand. He loved it.

We were walking up the street towards the Paradise Café with a whole crowd of people behind us. There were boys from Ewart's school asking him how many people had been killed, but Ewart didn't seem interested. He was dragging his feet.

'What's up?' I asked.

'It's me mam. She'll go ballistic.'

'Mine already has,' I said.

'Aye, but she's five hundred miles away and mine's only five doors up.'

'What're you going to tell her?'

'She'll already know. Everybody else does. Here, just in case I don't see you again.'

And he took a card out of his pocket and gave it to me. It was a picture of John Wayne, number thirty-two in a series of fifty, '*Stars Of The Silver Screen*'.

'It's no use putting it off,' said Uncle Gordon. 'Time to face the music. If you like I'll go in first and have a wee word.'

'Let me,' said Neville. 'It's the least I can do. She can't be that fierce.'

'You don't know her,' laughed Ewart.

We'd reached the door of the cafe. It looked deserted, the same way it had when I'd first arrived three days ago. Neville glanced up at the white lettering on the dark green paint work:

Paradise Café
(NO DIRTY BOOTS, NO WISECRACKS, NO DRUNKS!)

Proprietress: Eve Gunn

And he stopped dead.

'Is there something wrong?' asked Uncle Gordon.

'No,' whispered Neville, taking off his glasses and blinking, the way he always did when he was nervous or confused.

'Go on then. What're y'waiting for? A white flag? She's not going t'bite.'

Neville took a deep breath, put his glasses back on, pushed open the door and stepped inside. The tinkling of the tiny silver bells faded away and there was silence. A silence that seemed to reach out into the street and take your breath away. No-one moved. Then . . .

Crash! A large plate flew through the air and smashed on the far wall.

'Eve!'

Crash! Another plate.

'Wait! . . . I can explain.'

Crash!

'I didn't . . .'

Crash!

'Yooooou . . .' began Eve Gunn.

There were a few more smashed plates and a few moans and groans from Neville, as Ewart's mum's aim improved. Then Neville burst back out through the door, shielding his head with his arms. He backed into the middle of the street, followed by Ewart's mum, with her green eyes flashing and her red hair blazing and a stack of plates under her arm.

'Eve!' pleaded Neville.

'Yooooou . . .' began Ewart's mum all over again, and hurled the plates, one by one, with deadly accuracy, as he stumbled backwards down the main street towards the harbour. The shops had emptied and the streets were lined with people. There hadn't been a spectacle like this in Stromness for quite some time.

'Is there something I do not know about perhaps?' whispered Captain Allegretto.

'I've never seen her this bad,' muttered Ewart.

'Seems our Neville's having one of those days,' said Uncle Gordon, scratching at his red woollen hat.

We followed them at a safe distance. Ewart's mum had run out of plates and, although several women were offering her various items from their shopping bags such as boxes of eggs, tin cans and even the odd bottle, she was oblivious of the crowds. Neville was still walking backwards, pleading. Ewart's mum was marching forwards, pushing at his chest with her outstretched fingers, pushing him back out across the cobbled square, out to the very edge of the harbour.

'She's going to push him in!' said Ewart.

But then Neville grabbed her in a bear-hug and kissed her. Stromness held its breath. He stepped back, reached into his pocket and pulled out his ferry ticket. Ewart's mum looked at it for a couple of seconds then she looked at him. She stepped forward, took it off him, tore it up into little pieces and threw the pieces into the sea. Someone on the *St Ola* blew the ship's whistle and everyone cheered.

'And about time too,' said Uncle Gordon.

Ewart took his glasses off and blinked.

AN EPILOGUE

Strangers in the Night

'Was Granny very cross?' asked Sally.

'Only for a month or two,' laughed Uncle Stanley. 'Then Neville reappeared with Eve and Ewart and they smoothed things over.'

'Did they go and live in the Old Mill?'

'No, they moved down to London. All the publicity meant Neville's paintings were more in demand then ever. He became an instant celebrity: FAMOUS ARTIST COMES BACK FROM DEAD TO SAVE BOYS ON KILLER CLIFF

'My name was kept out of it as much as possible. Your gran thought I'd had enough excitement to last the summer. She was right.'

'What happened to the people in the gallery?'

'Well, the London police swooped down on Goldwater Fine Art. Donald Abercromby got five years, reduced to three for good behaviour. He now runs a small gallery selling pottery in the south of France. Patrick Fitzwilliam was never caught and has never been heard of since.'

'Is Uncle Gordon still alive?'

'No. Uncle Gordon died ten years ago, the year after I emigrated to New Zealand, but he must have been well into his nineties when he left.'

'Left?'

'Yes, he made what they call a "dramatic exit". Apparently he'd found an old World War Two mine washed up on the beach and for some daft reason he'd decided to cart it back up to The Eyrie. He was halfway up the path when it exploded. What was left of him was buried in the little cemetery at Rackwick. Neville carved the headstone. It's a three-foot-high granite glove. He wanted to paint it orange, but the minister disapproved. The Eyrie was left to Ewart.'

'Did Ewart become an astronaut?'

'No, but his lively imaginings eventually paid off. He's now a famous scriptwriter living in Hollywood, though he still goes back to Hoy once a year for a bit of peace and quiet, and to feed the cats.'

'Cats?'

'Yes. There's at least six. All wild. Wild and ginger like their grandfather. You see, Vincent didn't die, at least not when Elsie Robinson kicked his wicker basket off the clifftop. Either he got out before she arrived, or she coaxed him out, but the fact of the matter is that he marched into The Eyrie about three months after being abandoned. It must have been the smell of Uncle Gordon's fish pie. Uncle Gordon adopted him, but he was never what you'd call a domestic cat. He much preferred roaming the clifftops, hunting rabbits.'

'And Elsie Robinson, did they ever . . . ?'

'That's the strangest thing about this whole story. They searched for weeks, from one end of Hoy to the other, but they never found her body. It still makes me shudder. The thought that she might . . .'

There was a knocking at the door and a muffled voice shouted, 'It's only me. I forgot my key!'

'It's Gran,' said Sally.

'Coming, Mum!' shouted Uncle Stanley.

Sally didn't move. She stayed put on the sofa. She could hear her gran saying something about the rain starting up again and the phone lines being down, but Sally was only half there. She was half listening and half dreaming about the story. It was like being in two different places at once. Her eyes were looking at the wall, but her mind was looking at a beach, covered in huge round boulders and behind the boulders there were massive green and purple hills. And when she looked closer there was a boy on the beach. He was jumping from boulder to boulder.

Sally stood up and walked over to the sideboard, opened a drawer and lifted out the old photograph album that she'd been looking at the night before. She turned the stiff white pages until she found the two dog-eared photographs, John Wayne and Stanley Buckle, her uncle. She was still staring at the photograph when Gran and Uncle Stanley came into the room.

'I hear you two had an interesting afternoon,' said her gran.

'Yes,' said Sally, closing the album.

'Pity about the opening in London, though. Stanley was just telling me about the surprise he'd planned – to take you along. *That* would have been something to remember.'

'Oh, it doesn't matter,' said Sally. 'I've been to the Orkneys instead.'

Uncle Stanley smiled. 'Tell you what though, all that storytelling's given me an appetite. Does The Fox and Goose still do evening meals?'

'The best for miles around,' said Gran.

'Right then. I'll book a table for five, tonight at seven thirty. How's that sound?'

'It sounds lovely, dear, but I'm too tired to be bothered with going out again and David and Rachel aren't getting back till late. They've both gone straight to the meeting at the Village Hall. I think it would be nice if just the two of you went.'

'What do you think, Sally?' asked Uncle Stanley.

'Great. Are we getting dressed up?'

'You bet. Best bib and tucker.'

Sally ran out of the room and up the stairs.

'Won't Neville be expecting you?' Gran asked Uncle Stanley.

'He might have been. I wrote to him saying I was going to be there. But then, with the floods and all, he'll understand. I rang the gallery this morning and left another message saying I was stranded in Welford. He's that famous these days he'll not have time to worry about the likes of us. Besides, it's his big night. He's been waiting a long time for this and he's managed to stay alive long enough to enjoy it. Good luck to him.'

Sally had a bath, then went to her room and changed into the dress she saved for the most special occasions. It was only half past six – a whole hour to wait. She lay down on her bed and stared at the ceiling, counting ten backwards, which was what Gran always told her to do when she got too excited. She lay as still as possible, listening to the rain pattering on the window panes and the branches of the trees swishing in the wind outside. And she thought of Uncle Stanley and Ewart that first night on Hoy, when the storm was blowing over Uncle Gordon's house. And she thought of Uncle Gordon in his Eyrie and she felt sad that he was dead and that she'd never get to meet him. But then, she felt as though she *had* met him.

She'd met him with her uncle when he was telling her the story and sharing his memories. And she could 'see' Uncle Gordon, as if he'd been there, sitting on the chair in the corner of the room over by the window, with his beady black eyes shining like polished pebbles. He was rubbing the white stubble on his chin with his thick strong fingers and he was smiling. She watched as he stood up and went over to the window and looked out. And then, as Sally listened, the swishings and swayings and patterings seemed to merge into a single sound that grew louder and louder . . . CHOPCHOPCHOPCHOPCHOPCHOP CHOPCHOPCHOP!

She ran over to the window. But the window was just a black mirror, squirming with silver raindrops. She undid the latch and pushed it open. The wind and the rain blew into the room, scattering the curtains and throwing her hair back across her face. She pulled it aside and saw a bright light shining down from the sky on to the field at the bottom of their garden. The trees were swaying madly and in the dark sky there was an even darker shape – a *huge* shape – it was a helicopter!

Sally ran downstairs to the kitchen and flung open the back door. Gran joined her followed by Uncle Stanley, who'd just changed into his dinner jacket. They all stood in the doorway, staring into the darkness at the bottom of the garden. The din of the rotor blades died away leaving the murmur of the wind and the pattering of raindrops. Sally reached out and took hold of her uncle's hand, but without taking her eyes off the dark shape of the helicopter.

There were bits of voices being scattered in the wind and lights that flashed off and on. In the blackness of the far field, someone switched on a single bright light, a torch that began to move closer. It veered off to the right and disappeared behind next door's garden shed, but then retraced its steps and moved back left, to the bottom of Sally's garden. It skipped along the top of the fence and flew up amongst the tangled branches of the apple trees.

'Do you think they're lost?' asked Gran.

Uncle Stanley didn't reply. His eyes were fixed on the torch.

The beam fell out of the branches and landed on the old beehive, sitting square and white in the coal-black shadows. It lingered on the faded pink flower painted on the back, then turned and found the gate that opened on to the garden.

'They're coming in,' said Gran.

No-one moved. No-one said a thing. Sally felt her uncle's hand tighten round her own.

The garden gate creaked open and the glare of the torch hit their faces. Sally lifted a hand to shield her eyes but her uncle stepped forwards blocking the light. The torch was switched off and for a few seconds everything was blurry. Then Sally saw a big man in a brown overcoat. The overcoat was unbuttoned and underneath he was wearing a black suit, a white shirt and a red bow tie. His hair was longish and white and ruffled by the wind. When he pulled it out of his eyes you could see the big round 'owl' glasses and a smile that spread from ear to ear.

*

It looked like orange lemonade. It was called Buck's Fizz – champagne and fresh orange juice, mixed together and served in a champagne glass. Sally took a sip.

They left Neville surrounded by admirers and weaved their way through the crowds until, on the end wall of the end room, they found themselves standing in front of a very important painting.

Sally looked up at the bullet hole and then across

at Uncle Stanley. She didn't say anything, just leant her head against his arm and stared back at the painting. And as she stared the swirls of green became the sea, and the splodges of red became the rock, and the chatter of the people faded away as she stood on the edge of the cliff listening to the whistling wind and the screaming gulls.

'Don't stand too close,' said Uncle Stanley. 'Remember the puffins!'

THE END

THE GIANT GOLDFISH ROBBERY
Richard Kidd

Forget Moby Dick . . . Forget the great, white whale . . . These were the great orange whales. A whole pondful!

Moving home has not been much fun for Jimmy and his family, least of all for his fisherman father who has had to leave behind the sea and his treasured boat.

Then, out of the blue, Jimmy meets Major Gregory, an elderly gentleman and prize collector of koi carp. Soon Jimmy is hooked and wants to learn everything there is to know about these gentle orange giants. But before long he finds himself in deep – and very dangerous – water.

SHORTLISTED FOR THE BRANFORD BOASE AWARD 2000

'The best adventure story for seven- to ten-year-olds so far this year'
Literary Review

'A witty contemporary adventure story'
Financial Times

0 440 86412 7

CORGI YEARLING BOOKS

THE DREAM-MASTER
Theresa Breslin

'There are always rules . . . I am the Dream Master. Not you. What I say goes. And I say this dream is gone, so beat it.'

There are good dreams and there are rotten dreams, but once they're over, they're over. Or are they? For one morning, as Cy is about to wake up from a terrific dream about Ancient Egypt, he discovers that he *can* get back into his dream world. There's just one problem: the Dream Master, who isn't used to stroppy boys standing up to him and wanting to break all the rules. And as Cy moves back and forth between the present day and the land of the pharaohs – sorting out all kinds of problems with schoolwork and bullies – dream life and real life become ingeniously intertwined!

'Engaging fantasy . . . treads assuredly the line between thrills and laughs'
The Observer

0 440 863821

CORGI YEARLING BOOKS

All Transworld titles are available by post from:

Bookpost
PO Box 29
Douglas
Isle of Man IM99 1BQ

Tel: +44(0)1624 836000
Fax: +44(0)1624 837033
Internet http://www.bookpost.co.uk
or e-mail: bookshop@enterprise.net

Free postage and packing in the UK.
Overseas customers: allow £1 per book
(paperbacks) and £3 per book (hardbacks).